The Middle of Somewhere

A RICHARD JACKSON BOOK

The Middle of Somewhere

A Story of South Africa

Sheila Gordon

Orchard Books   New York

Orchard Books, A division of Franklin Watts, Inc.
387 Park Avenue South, New York, NY 10016

Manufactured in the United States of America
Book design by Mina Greenstein
The text of this book is set in 12 pt. Garamond No. 3
2 4 6 8 10 9 7 5 3 1

Library of Congress Cataloging-in-Publication Data
Gordon, Sheila. The middle of somewhere / by Sheila Gordon.
p. cm. "A Richard Jackson book"—Half t.p.
Summary: Nine-year-old Rebecca and her family, living in a South
African village for black people, are threatened with forced removal to a
bleak, distant development, to make room for a new suburb for whites.
ISBN 0-531-05908-1. ISBN 0-531-08508-2 (lib. bdg.)
[1. South Africa—Race relations—Fiction. 2. Blacks—South Africa—
Fiction. 3. Race relations—Fiction.]
I. Title. PZ7.G65937Mi 1990 [Fic]—dc20
90-30625 CIP AC

To the children
of the three and a half million black South
Africans who have been involuntarily or forcibly
removed from their homes under the government's
policy of reserving certain areas of the country
for whites only

1

REBECCA took her doll's clothes off the wash line. They smelled fresh, full of the wind and hot sunshine that had dried them. She sat down on the hard ground and dressed the doll, braiding its scrappy hair and tying the braids with bits of string. Though it was rather battered and the pink and white paint of its face crackled, the doll's blue eyes opened and shut and it cried "Mama" when it was tipped over.

Rebecca's friend Noni, sitting beside her, asked, "What are you going to call her?"

"Betty." Rebecca placed the doll carefully in its shoe-box bed, and the eyes closed. "You can cover her now, Noni. Here's the sheet." She handed her friend a large white handkerchief, then a piece of an old, frayed blanket.

Noni tucked the doll in. "It's a shame they didn't take care of her properly. She's pretty."

They looked down at it sleeping in the box. "Never

mind," Rebecca said. "If her face wasn't cracked and her hair nearly all pulled out, they wouldn't have given her to me. And her clothes are nice."

Noni lifted the covers. "We've put her to bed with her shoes on!"

They both laughed. "I'm afraid they'll get lost if I take them off," Rebecca explained.

The two girls were playing in the feathery shade of a jacaranda tree that had taken root and grown tall in the patch of yard in front of Rebecca's house. The house, a small brick dwelling with a flat tin roof, was one of many crowded close together in a South African village for black people on a stretch of rolling *veld* surrounded by low hills called *koppies*. From the top of the *koppie* where she and her friends sometimes played, the ramshackle huddle of houses —some of brick, others of corrugated iron and scrap wood—seemed to Rebecca nothing more than a smudge of dirt and smoke on the coarse, sun-yellowed grass.

But as soon as she came indoors, the two-roomed house with its familiar smell of kerosene fuel and *putu*—the cornmeal porridge her granny cooked on the two-burner primus stove—was a comfort. From the hilltop, under the huge sky, blue and cloudless, it was a small, mean house; but when she went in through the door, it was home.

"Your turn now." She took the doll from the box and handed it to her friend.

Noni tipped it over. "Mama," the doll cried. "Oh—why are you crying, Betty?" Noni crooned. Holding it in her arms, she rocked the doll to and fro and sang a little *Xhosa* lullaby.

"She's crying because she's sad," Rebecca said. "She's crying because she knows you want to move away to Pofadderkloof."

"You *know* I don't want to move, Rebecca," Noni said. "But that man from the planning department told my mother and father we have to. We'll *all* have to. He says black people can't live in this village anymore. They're going to build a new town here for white people. But he said the houses at Pofadderkloof are much better than what we have now. They're all brand-new, he says. We'll have our own water tap right in the house. And Rebecca—there'll be *electric light* in all the houses."

Rebecca took the doll back and tucked it firmly under the blanket. Not looking at her friend she said, "My father says it's all lies—just to get us to move. He doesn't believe anything that man told him. My Granny says we belong here and we're staying."

"But *Rebecca*—they're going to come with bulldozers and run backward and forward until *everything* is all flat—our houses, beds, tables, chairs—*everything*." Noni spread her hands out flat and her voice rose high with dismay.

While her friend was speaking, Rebecca saw the

3

box with her doll in it leveled out, pressed down into one flat piece as if an elephant had trod on it. Her face set with a stubborn look. "They want us to think that to frighten us," she said, echoing her father's words. "My parents say if we just stay, and say we won't go, they can't send bulldozers to flatten houses that are full of people."

"But doesn't that make you scared?" Noni asked.

Rebecca folded the top of the doll's sheet over the blanket, not answering. It was better not to think about it; thinking about it did make her scared.

"Good evening, children."

They looked up to see Mr. Lekota, the preacher, in his long black robe and white collar, the round toes of his big black boots dusty from the red dirt road.

"Good evening, Mr. Lekota," they chorused.

"Playing with your dolly? Good girls." He smiled down at them. "Everything all right with you?"

"Mr. Lekota," Noni blurted out, "isn't it true that they'll come and bulldoze our houses if we don't move?"

The preacher stopped smiling. "Now don't you worry your little heads about such things," he said. "Do your lessons and help your mothers and play with your dollies, and leave us to deal with those who wish to do us harm." He patted their heads and walked on down the road.

Noni started to say something, but the look on Rebecca's face stopped her.

4

"*Noni* . . ." Her mother was calling from the house next door. She appeared in the doorway with the baby slung on her back in a shawl. "Your father will be home soon. Come and take care of the little ones for me so that I can get the food on the stove."

Noni stood up. She brushed down her short, faded cotton frock and wiggled her bare toes in the warm red dust. She looked longingly at Betty snug in her box.

"I'll lend her to you tomorrow," Rebecca said. "You can keep her the whole night."

"The whole night!"

Rebecca nodded. The two friends smiled at each other.

"*Noni! Are you coming?*" her mother's voice shrilled out.

"See you tomorrow." Noni hurried home.

In the box Betty lay asleep, her long stiff eyelashes against her crackled cheeks; Rebecca picked it up and went indoors.

2

IT WAS A Thursday, Rebecca's favorite day of the week, because on Thursdays her mother had the afternoon off. Mama worked and lived in the town as cook and housekeeper in a white suburb, a two-hour bus ride from the village. Every Thursday, and every second Sunday, she was given time off to spend the afternoon and night with her family. She would have to get up early the next morning, before it was light, to be back at work in time to have breakfast ready when the white family woke up.

Today she had brought the doll for Rebecca; her madam—the white woman she worked for—had been clearing out her daughter's toy cupboard and had said she could take the doll home. Inside the small house, her mother was preparing green beans for supper, and Rebecca slipped onto her lap, leaning comfortably against her. Her mother hugged her and went on snapping the tips off the beans, working with her arms around the child.

Rebecca took the doll from its box and sat it on her knees. "Now I'm on your lap, and Betty's on *my* lap."

"You've named her Betty?"

Rebecca nodded. She felt safe here; with the warmth and strength of her mother against her back it didn't seem possible that anyone could come and bulldoze their house down. On the primus stove the cornmeal porridge bubbled while her grandmother stirred. This evening there was a good smell of stewing meat as well. Her mother had brought a bag of meaty lamb bones, and as they simmered in the pot with onions and carrots, Rebecca felt her stomach growl at the thought of the meal they would be having.

She listened to the sound of her mother and grandmother talking, but not their words. With Betty on her lap and the good smell of the food, she felt drowsy with contentment in the familiar room that served as kitchen, living room, dining room, and even, at night, bedroom; at bedtime a flowered curtain strung from the ceiling would be drawn around the couch in the corner to form a tiny sleeping area for Granny. Rebecca shared the small adjoining bedroom with her parents and her brother, John. There was no bathroom—just a privy at the back of the house and a public tap that they shared with the neighbors.

Granny kept the house spotless. There were yellow-and-white striped curtains at the windows; blue patterned linoleum was on the floor. Pots and pans and dishes were neatly stored on shelves Rebecca's father had put up; cups hung from hooks in a row. Granny had covered the shelves and kitchen table with red and blue checkered oilcloth. And on a windowsill a pot of pink flowers bloomed; the gardener at the house where Rebecca's mother worked had given it to her; he said they were called geraniums. *Everything has a name*, Rebecca thought—flowers . . . geraniums; her doll . . . Betty. . . . *Pofadderkloof*. Drowsing, she had been slipping off her mother's lap, but at the thought of Pofadderkloof she jerked into wakefulness and sat up with a start. The man from the government office had told them that the houses at Pofadderkloof were new, with running water and electricity . . . but they couldn't be as snug and cheerful as this, Rebecca felt sure.

Her brother John came in at the door that stood open to the bright warm evening.

"How are you, my boy?" Mama asked.

"Hullo, Mama." He sat down on the couch, took a comic book from his pocket, unrolled it, and looked at it without answering.

Rebecca wriggled off her mother's lap. At the sight of her brother's glum face her contentment fell away. "Look at my new doll, John," she said. She went over to show it to him. "Her name is Betty. Mama's madam sent it to me for a present."

He looked up from his comic book. "That's not a new doll. It's an old broken doll. Look at it—all cracks on its face—hardly any hair. That's not a present. It's rubbish." He made as if to grab it. "Give it to me and I'll throw it in the rubbish bin for you."

Rebecca stepped back. She clutched Betty close, protecting her.

"Leave the child alone," Granny scolded. "She likes the doll."

Rebecca wished that her mother had brought a present for John. It might cheer him up. He was always in a bad mood these days. She knew he was sad and ashamed because he wasn't allowed to go to school. *It's not fair*, she thought. John was fourteen, five years older than she. The new term had begun a few weeks ago, but their school was so overcrowded and so short of desks and pencils and books that the school principal had said he was very sorry but he had room only for children with passing grades. And since John hadn't done so well last term, he was among those who would have to stay home and do their lessons on their own.

"Come here, my boy."

Reluctantly, John rose and went to stand by his mother. She put her arm around him. "I know you're feeling bad, Johnny. But listen—tonight your father and I are going to a meeting at the church hall, organized by Big Albert Kosane. People from the education department will be there. And we're going to talk with them about all of you who are being kept out of school."

"It won't make any difference," John blurted.

9

"*They* don't care what happens to us. They don't care if we become *tsotsis*. Maybe I should become a *tsotsi* —they always have money in their pockets. If I'm not allowed in school at least I could have money to buy things!"

Granny turned from the stove and shook her wooden spoon pasted white with cornmeal at him. "Don't let me hear you talk like that, my boy! You're not too big for me to thrash you."

"He doesn't mean it," their mother said. "He knows the *tsotsis* are a bad, dangerous lot—smoking and drinking, never going to school and getting in trouble all the time. *Listen* to me, Johnny. A lot of parents are coming tonight. You'll see—something will be done. Try to stop feeling so bad and go and fill up the water bucket for Granny. Rebecca—you can set the table. And look in that blue plastic bag. I brought back a nice piece of cake and some jam tarts. They had a card party last night and my madam always makes me bake too much, so she said I should take what was left over."

Rebecca put her doll away in its box in the bed-room. "Be good and sleep now, Betty," she whispered. "I'll see you later." She set the table and put the cake and jam tarts on a blue tin plate, glad to see that the cake was chocolate with a thick layer of buttery icing.

She was hungry. "I'll go out and meet Papa," she told her mother. Above the hills, great masses of

10

pearly cloud were piling up as the night fog rolled in from the ocean. At the corner of the dusty road the blue *kombis*—minibuses in which people rode to and from work—were pulling in and unloading passengers. Swinging on the gate, Rebecca saw her father at last. "Papa! Papa! I've got a new doll," she called. "And there's stewed lamb and chocolate cake for supper."

Her father lifted her up and hugged her. These days he was in a good mood when she ran to meet him. She remembered how he used to come home late and weary when he took the regular bus, having stood nearly all the way after a long wait in the endless bus line. But now, since people in the village had started to run their own minibuses which left frequently, traveling to town and back was cheaper and not so hard on him. He worked at the Ace Supermarket, unloading crates of groceries from trucks, stamping the prices on them, and stacking them on shelves. On Fridays he would bring home food that he was able to buy cheaply because the cans were dented, wrappings damaged, fruit and vegetables bruised.

But today was Thursday. Mama's day. Hand in hand, Rebecca and her father walked home.

3

WHEN REBECCA woke next morning her mother had already left for work. Her father was at the table with John, where Granny was serving them their breakfast.

"Why do I have to be up so early when I can't even go to school?" John grumbled. His shirt was unbuttoned and he looked cross and sleepy.

"I can't let you lie in bed all day," Granny said. "It's not good for you. You can help around the house. I'm an old woman and I get tired." She moved briskly from stove to table, thin and full of energy, pouring mugs of tea, cutting bread. She didn't look old or tired to Rebecca.

"Don't you want to know what happened at the meeting last night, John?" Papa asked.

"Nothing, I suppose."

"Wrong, my boy. Quite wrong. Many people came—so many . . . the church hall was packed. Standing room only. People are angry about their kids being kept out of school. Those men from the education department, they came there thinking they were just going to smooth things over—tell us about the wonderful new school there would be at Pofadderkloof, then send us all home. Well—they soon found out they were mistaken." He laughed. "When they felt the anger in that hall they stopped smiling—their faces turned quite pale."

"So what are they going to do then?" John asked.

Rebecca, watching her brother, saw how anxious and eager he looked.

"What about *now*?" Granny demanded. "What about this child? How long must he sit at home?"

"Wait, Granny," Papa said, "let me finish. That's what everyone in the hall began to shout: *What about now! What about now!* People were standing on the benches, shaking their fists! You should have seen those white officials—they were really scared." He laughed again; shook his head. "At last, Big Albert Kosane stood up on a chair and quieted the crowd. He told those white men that we will keep all our children home from school unless something is done *right now* to admit those being kept out." He spread apricot jam from a dented tin over his bread. Three pairs of eyes were on him as he bit, chewed and swallowed, drank some tea.

"And *then*?" John asked.

"Then," Papa went on, "those white men huddled together for a while on the platform. Then they asked

Big Albert to come up and talk with them. Then they announced that they'll send *another teacher*. And those who have been kept out can come back. You'll have your lessons under the trees in the school yard, Johnny."

"Under the trees . . . ?" John said doubtfully.

"Oh well—at least that'll be better than packed in that crowded classroom." But Rebecca could see he wasn't really pleased.

"Don't think that will be an excuse for fooling around," Granny warned him.

John stood, buttoned his shirt, tucked it into his pants. "So I can go back today, Papa?"

"Wait—wait. Not so fast. It will take a few days, my boy. Until the new teacher comes. You can stop feeling sorry for yourself now." Papa stood up to leave. "Keep studying your schoolbooks on your own until then."

"What else can I do?" John complained. "Granny won't let me out of the house until school's out."

"Do what your granny tells you. She brought your mother up right. She knows what she's doing." He patted John's shoulder, tipped Rebecca's chin, and went off to where the *kombis* were waiting.

NONI'S HEAD appeared in the doorway. "Are you coming, Rebecca?" she called.

"One minute." Rebecca ran to the bedroom to fetch her schoolbag. She took her sleeping doll out of the shoe box and sat her up on the bed against the pillow. The blue eyes opened and looked at her. "See you after school, Betty." Calling good-bye to Granny and John, she hurried out the door.

This morning her heart felt lighter. Every day when she went off to school leaving John sitting sadly at the breakfast table, she felt as if there was a stone lodged in the place where her heart was supposed to be. She would walk along the dusty road, quiet, not responding to Noni's chatter; it was as though she had been given a plate of food while her brother remained hungry. Whenever she thought of him stuck in the house every day, alone with Granny, she wasn't able to enjoy lessons or playtime.

Today she went along with such a quick, light step that Noni had to hurry to keep up. "Why are you walking so fast?" she asked. "We're not late— there's plenty of time."

Rebecca hugged her good news to herself. She didn't want to talk about it to Noni because she didn't want her to know how bad she'd been feeling for her brother.

She slowed her pace, swinging her schoolbag and watching the dark blue of her shadow as it moved lightly over the mud puddles beside the public tap; it went dancing alongside her over the stony rubble that lay on the dirt road, turned wavy as it glanced over a corrugated iron fence, kept company with her in the hot, clear light of the early morning.

"My granny says when she has the time she'll make a nightie for Betty on her sewing machine," she told Noni as they neared school. "Then she won't have to go to bed in her clothes."

"Tonight?" Noni wailed. "Will she sew it tonight? You said I could borrow Betty tonight—you promised."

"She won't sew it tonight. Sometime—when she's not busy. You can borrow Betty this evening. I said you could, didn't I?"

BUT IN the late afternoon, when Noni came to fetch Betty, Rebecca wished that she hadn't promised to lend her. With a pang she handed over the doll in the shoe box. "Don't let your little brothers get their hands on her, Noni. They might smash her."

"Oh, don't worry; I won't let them *touch* her," Noni promised. "I'll just show them how her eyes open and close and how she says *Mama*. And when I'm not playing with her I'll put her on top of the wardrobe where they can't reach. I want to show her to my auntie Miriam, too. Thanks, Rebecca." She walked slowly back to her house, her eyes on the doll as she went.

Rebecca did homework until suppertime. Papa was pleased when Granny told him that John had worked all morning at his schoolbooks, and supper was more cheerful than it had been for a while, though not as pleasant as when Mama was home. "I wish Mama could be here every night," she said.

16

"What's the matter with those white people?" John burst out, angry suddenly. "Why can't they cook their own food and wash their own dishes!"

"They pay your mother good wages to live in," Papa told him. "Or else where would we get the money for your school fees, your books, your clothes. Everything is so dear."

"Joshua Kosane told me that white kids don't have to pay for school or books. *They* get it all for free."

"Eat your *putu* before it gets cold," Granny said. "You should be thankful your parents both have jobs and we have enough to eat." Deftly, she sopped the sauce in her plate with a scoop of the grainy white porridge.

"Anyway, she's off this Sunday," Papa remarked. "Only two more days."

In bed that night, Rebecca felt lonely without her doll. She wondered how she was getting along at Noni's house. She hoped those wild little brothers wouldn't get their hands on her.

4

"MAKE SURE you cut exactly along the lines, child." It was a few weeks later, and Granny was showing Rebecca how to make clothes for Betty. With a black crayon she drew the patterns for Betty's nightie on a sheet of newspaper for Rebecca to cut out. Then she pinned the shapes onto pieces of fabric from the bag of brightly colored ends and scraps of cloth she had saved. She never threw anything away. "Every little thing is useful for something," she always said. Rebecca watched as Granny skillfully cut the cloth into backs and fronts and sleeves for a dress as well as the nightie.

"Where did you learn to sew, Granny?"

"When I used to work in town, I would go on my afternoon off to a nearby church where there were classes for black domestic workers. They taught reading, writing, knitting, sewing, cooking. First I learned to read. Then I took the sewing course. I really enjoyed sewing, and I found I was good at it.

So I saved up money for a long, long time, and at last I bought this sewing machine." She earned money dressmaking and altering clothes for women in the village, and sometimes, when she was not too busy, she would make clothes for Rebecca.

While she spoke she ran the cutout pieces under the whirring needle, stitching them together with narrow, even seams. She snipped off the thread and turned the garment right-side out, smoothed it flat, and there was a perfect little yellow nightie for Betty, with a ruffle around the hem.

"Oh Granny, it's beautiful."

"See if it fits."

Rebecca undressed Betty and was slipping the nightie over the doll's head when Noni walked in.

"Noni. Come and see the nightie Granny has just made for Betty."

Noni stood by the table, watching, saying nothing.

"It fits just right. Look, Noni, it even has a ruffle."

Still Noni remained silent.

"What's the matter with you, child?" Granny asked. "Did a monkey run away with your tongue?"

Noni sat down. "We're going to move," she said gravely.

"Move!" Rebecca put the doll down on the table. "To Pofadderkloof?"

Noni nodded.

Saying the name—Pofadderkloof—gave Rebecca

a strange feeling, as if her heart were growing a little smaller.

"So your parents have decided?" Granny asked.

Again, Noni nodded. "My mother told me when I walked in from school," she said. "Those two men from the planning department came again last night. They talked to my mother and father and Auntie Miriam for a long time. They told them that everyone will *have* to move. Even those who say they won't go. . . . Then—then the whole village is going to be bulldozed. But if we go first we can choose one of the nicer houses at Pofadderkloof."

Rebecca and Granny said nothing.

Noni went on. "And the men said to my mother—they said, 'Look how crowded it is here with four children and your sister all living one on top of the other, some sleeping on the floor.' They said if we move we'll have a bigger house, with *two* bedrooms, with a plot of ground where we can plant a garden. *Mealies*, he said, and tomatoes, and maybe flowers. . . ." In the silence, her voice faltered and petered out.

"*Ha!*" Granny slammed the cover shut over her machine. She gathered up the scraps of cloth, tidied away the scissors and spools of thread. Rebecca saw her face was angry. Sadly she thought, *Now she's not going to sew the dress she's cut out for Betty.*

"Go and play outside, children." She flapped her hands at them. "You're under my feet. I haven't got time to waste—I've got a lot to do. Outside, now —both of you."

Taking Betty with them, the girls went and sat down in the shade of the jacaranda. No one had planted the jacaranda tree. It was just there. Rebecca's mother had said that maybe, a long time ago, the wind had blown a seed to this spot; or perhaps a seed had dropped here from the beak of a bird. It had taken root when Mama was a small child. At first Granny had thought the sprout was a weed; but then she said it looked too tough, too strong, as if it had thoughts of bigger things than being a weed. So she had left it to grow. Now it was taller than the house, with feathery fronds of deep green. In early summer it was covered with a mass of blue-mauve blossoms. As the summer went on they would come drifting down slowly to the ground until it looked as if a small blue lake were lapping around the trunk. The blossoms were like narrow, frilled bells. They felt like a piece of velvet Granny had once sewn a dress from. Rebecca and Noni would fit them like gloves over their fingertips or thread them into necklaces and bracelets.

The two friends had played under the tree since they first started to walk. They had both been born here, in the village, only two weeks apart. They were in the same class at school and played together every day. Just as the jacaranda tree had always been there, so had Noni always been there. *And now . . .* Rebecca thought . . . *Noni is going to go away . . . to Pofadderkloof*. In the silence under the tree, she took the yellow nightie off the doll and dressed her in her clothes. When she had buttoned on both of the tiny black plastic shoes, without looking up, she spoke at last.

"You're really going to live there . . . in that . . . place." *Pofadderkloof*. It was as if her tongue couldn't get around that name and it stuck, hard and dry, in her mouth.

"Rebecca. Don't look so fierce. It will be better than here—you'll see. Look how ugly and poor everything is here. There it will be all new, and clean, and nice. There'll be a new school, and a clinic, and a nursery school for my little brothers, the man told us. It will be better for *everybody*."

"Who will I have for a friend when you go?"

"Rebecca. *Listen to me.* You're going to have to move too. They're going to bulldoze this place. There'll be *nothing* here. We'll be together there—at—"

"At *Pofadderkloof*!" She spat out the name as if ridding her mouth of it.

"Yes."

Rebecca packed her doll clothes into the box and stood up. Without another word she ran indoors.

Noni sat for a few moments, alone under the jacaranda tree, frowning in bewilderment. Then she stood up and walked slowly back to her own house.

INSIDE, Rebecca found Granny sitting at the table reading the Bible. It was thick, covered in dark blue cloth, with tiny print. Her lips moved as, line by line, her finger slowly traced the words.

Rebecca sat on the couch with her doll. She knew better than to interrupt when Granny was reading the Bible. She undid Betty's braids and tied her hair back in a tail.

John came in with some comic books. He sat down beside her. "D'you want to look at one?"

"No thanks. They're full of fighting."

"What would you like them to be about—*dolls*?"

Rebecca laid Betty on her lap. *Mama*, the doll cried, closing her eyes. It was quiet in the house. There were the familiar sounds of the clock on the sideboard ticking peacefully, Granny murmuring as she read, John turning the pages. A beam of late afternoon sun at the window lit up the geraniums so that they glowed like pink lanterns. But the name her tongue didn't want to form kept rising in her mind, spoiling everything.

"John," Rebecca said.

"Mm-hm?"

"What kind of snake is a *pofadder*?"

"*Pofadder*? A very bad kind. Their necks puff up, like balloons, before they bite." He formed his thumb and forefinger into a snake head, snapping them at her. "Bite you—you die."

23

"Are they very big?"

"Small."

"How small?"

"About half as long as this comic book. Thin as my finger." He went on reading.

Rebecca liked the sound of the clock. Sometimes, when she woke in the middle of the night, she would hear it comfortably ticking away, *tick-tock, tick-tock*; it would lull her back to sleep. . . . John was in a better mood these days, since he had gone back to school. . . . But yesterday, she had passed him in the school yard, sitting on the ground under the trees waiting for lessons to begin. He was watching his friends as they lined up to go into the classroom, and the look on his face had made her feel very sad. *Tick-tock, tick-tock* . . . each tick of the clock was like a small hammer beat of trouble.

Saturday today . . . Mama would be here tomorrow. . . . Rebecca held Betty in her arms, rocking her.

At last Granny closed the Bible, put it away at the bottom of the wardrobe, and began to cook the *putu* for supper.

5

ON SUNDAY MORNING Rebecca took Betty outside to wait for her mother's bus to arrive from town. The bus stop was in front of the church at the end of their road. A boy came running by, rolling a car tire, keeping it balanced by means of two wooden rods. He was chased by two smaller boys who shouted out, "Watch where you're going, Rebecca—or the bulldozer will roll you flat!" Across the road on an empty patch of ground used as a soccer field, John was kicking a ball around with his friends.

She saw the bus pull in and her mother step down, and went running to meet her. At the sight of Mama in her navy-blue dress and maroon beret, her bulky plastic shopping bag bulging, her smooth round face smiling, Rebecca's troubles fell away like mud washed off by running water. All night she had dreamed of snakes—a bare rocky place with snakes sliding about, rearing up, hissing. No houses or people, only snakes. And rocks. Now, as her mother hugged her and they walked hand in hand to the house, she forgot her bad dreams. John waved and called a greeting from the soccer field.

Mama's shopping bag was full of good things: oranges, bananas, a chicken for dinner; and some secondhand books for John and Rebecca which she had bought at a church sale.

In the drowsy summer afternoon, flies buzzed on the windowpanes; a butterfly, looking in vain for a garden, lighted on the pot of geraniums at the open window and settled, delicately prodding at the sweetness it found inside the flowers.

Soon, the house filled with the good smell of stewing chicken. Papa, in the one comfortable chair, read out items from the Sunday paper while Mama cooked and Granny, at the sewing machine, finished off a dress she was making for Noni's auntie Miriam, who was very pretty and loved having new clothes.

Rebecca looked at one of the books Mama had brought. It was a story about children who lived in a place where it snowed. There were pictures of houses, streets, trees, all covered over in white, children playing in it, throwing balls of it at each other. She had never seen snow. She looked up from the page, watching the butterfly as it pranced lightly in the flowers, wondering what snow was like . . . how did it feel to press it into balls, to walk on it? . . . cold and white and soft. Perhaps it was like walking on soft ice cream? . . .

John was poring over a brightly colored picture

book about space travel. "It says here that there are a hundred thousand million stars in the sky."

"My word," Granny murmured as she treadled away at the sewing machine. "How do they manage to count them all?"

There were footsteps out in the yard. Through the window Rebecca could see Mr. and Mrs. Mkwane, Noni's parents, coming toward the door. Her heart stiffened. She felt the trouble starting up again.

MR. AND MRS. MKWANE came in and sat down at the kitchen table. Granny finished the seam she was sewing, snapped off the thread, and got up to put the kettle on to boil for tea for the visitors. Mr. Mkwane looked gravely at Papa. "They came again to talk to us last night, brother," he said.

"From the planning committee?" Papa asked.

Mr. Mkwane nodded. "Now . . . my wife and I . . . since we got out of bed this morning it's been nothing but argue and discuss, discuss and argue—what to do—to move?—to stay?"

"We want to talk it over with you," Mrs. Mkwane said.

Papa folded his newspaper, flattening the folds with his fingertips again and again. Mama lowered the flame under the pot and sat down. John closed his book. Rebecca went to stand beside Mama, leaning in the curve of her arm. Except for the bubbling of the chicken stew, there was silence in the room.

Mrs. Mkwane spoke. She was a thin woman who

always looked worried. "I can't get it out of my mind," she said, "the thought of a nice house, like they told us, two bedrooms, electric lights, a sink in the kitchen with running water. My back always hurts from carrying heavy buckets of water. . . . Ever since they told me about the houses at Pofadderkloof, our house seems to have grown even smaller—so cramped, so crowded. I can't stand it any longer—my sister Miriam, the four kids, all of us one on top of the other, no place to put anything. . . ." Her chin was trembling, her fingers wringing a small red handkerchief. "It would be better for all of us—for the whole village—we should all move there."

"Tell me—what's the good of a nice house if it's three hours from town?" Papa asked. "Even if they build me a palace there, how am I going to get to work? I can't travel six hours every day to and from my job." He lifted his hand toward Mama. "As for her—half the time on her day off would be spent on the bus."

Rebecca recognized the grim look on his face—like the time he had heard that Uncle Sizwe had been killed in an accident on the building site where he'd been working.

"The man told us there will be jobs at Pofadderkloof," Mrs. Mkwane insisted.

"What kind of jobs, out there in the middle of nowhere?" Mama asked with scorn.

"They told us a fruit-canning factory is going to be built there," Mr. Mkwane said.

"Even if there are going to be some jobs," Papa said, "I've been working fifteen years at the supermarket. There's my pension, my promotion. I lose all of that if I leave. It's no use." He shook his head. "We can't go."

"I am born here," Granny stated flatly. "Sixty-two years I am here. Here I stay."

Rebecca saw Granny had turned off the kettle. She wasn't going to offer the Mkwanes a cup of tea now.

From the sofa John spoke in a tight, angry voice. "How can you let those white men push you around, tell you *where* you must go, *what* you must do!"

"Ssh, John. Where are your manners?" Papa reprimanded him. He drummed his fingers for a while on the wooden arm of the chair, concentrating, as though he were doing a hard sum in his head. In the quietness the clock ticked loudly. "You know something," he said at last, "maybe the boy is right. After all—why *should* we pack up and go just because they tell us—"

"Just because they want to build a nice, new suburb for whites here, you mean," John interrupted.

"Johnny . . ." Mama said warningly.

"I can't stand this arguing and discussing any longer!" Mrs. Mkwane stood up. "It's too much for me."

Her husband, with an apologetic shrug, followed her out of the house.

EVEN THOUGH the dinner was delicious, with plenty of gravy to scoop up with *putu*, Rebecca ate with little appetite. It was as though the *pofadders* had escaped from her dream to lurk in cracks and corners of the house, unseen, waiting to puff up and strike. The talk around the table was nothing but Pofadderkloof . . . Pofadderkloof . . .

"Let those Mkwanes go if they want," Granny said. "We stay."

In a small voice Rebecca said, "But they'll come with bulldozers—and knock our house down—and flatten everything. . . ."

"Oh," Papa said, "they only say that to try and force us to go."

"How do you know they won't?" Mama asked. "They've done it in other places."

"They work on people like the Mkwanes next door," Papa told her. "They try to scare them. They think if they can get a few families to move, others will follow them."

But Rebecca could see that even though Papa was talking bravely, he looked as worried as Mama.

John had been eating steadily, not joining in the discussion. "My granny has been living here sixty-two years," he burst out, "and now they're coming to chase us away so that white people can come and live here." With the knife he had been using to spread margarine on his bread, he made a slashing gesture that cut through the air. "I *hate* those people—*hate* them!"

Mama took the knife from him and put it down on the table, gently clasping his wrist in her large hand. "Ssh . . . Johnny. Don't talk that way, my boy. Hate is wrong."

"Pushing people out of their homes is wrong," he retorted with anger.

Rebecca got up from the table, went to the bedroom, and came back with Betty. She held her on her lap, feeling afraid; there was no safe place for them. She smoothed the hair back from Betty's forehead.

"Eat your food, child, don't play," Granny admonished.

But it was hard for Rebecca to swallow.

A loud knocking on the door startled her. A booming voice called out. The door opened and in came Big Albert Kosane. "Ah—the whole Gwala family's home. Good!"

"Albert! Come in."

"Welcome, brother. Take a seat."

"Come and share a meal with us."

A chair was pulled up for him, a plate filled with food. Big Albert Kosane, a large good-humored man with a hearty laugh, worked in the town as a mechanic in a garage. He was head of the village council and people with trouble always went to him for help.

With him sitting in it the small room seemed even smaller; but it seemed that Big Albert could protect them from harm. He ate with great appetite, his deep voice rising from the huge barrel of his chest. "I bet you I know what you were talking about before I came," he said.

"Pofadderkloof," John said resentfully.

"Right, Johnny! It's the same in every house I've been to." He stripped the meat off a chicken leg. "Those baboons from the planning department have been going from house to house ahead of me, trying to scare our people into moving."

"Albert," Mama said. "What's going to happen about this black spot?"

"Black spot!" Rebecca exclaimed. She looked around the room. "Where? What black spot?"

"A black spot, my child," Big Albert explained, "is when the government wants to use our land for settling white people. This place, our village, is a black spot, the government says. It's nice here— good land with the hills all around, and not too far from town. They want to build a new suburb here, for white people. And we have to be moved somewhere else, they say."

"Do they think we are weeds they can pull up and throw away?" Granny said. "We have deep roots— like trees. We were always here; long before the white people came with their talk of *black spots*, we were here. My grandmother lived here. . . ."

"Right, Granny," Big Albert said. "Here we are and here we *stay*." His voice vibrated among the pots and pans on the shelves.

They were all silent, waiting while he drank a gulp of tea, placed his mug on the table, looked around at all of them.

"*We stay*." He spoke slowly, firmly. "If every one of us refuses to budge, what can they do? They can't go around destroying houses with people in them. We already have some lawyers working on our case. The important thing is for all of us to stick together. Together, we can hold on to what is rightfully ours and has been ours for generations." He held out his hand as if it enclosed the whole village.

"But my friend Noni next door—her family *is* moving," Rebecca piped up.

Albert's great laugh boomed out. He lightly lifted her from her chair and swung her onto his lap. "Oh, I see you have a dolly hiding under the table. What's her name?"

"Betty."

"Well, you can tell Betty from me that we won't give in as easily as they think. We'll fight to keep our village. I'll be on my way next door now, and I'll explain our plan to Noni's family, little one."

"Do they give you supper at every house you go to?" Granny asked.

Rebecca felt Big Albert's laughter quivering through her. "Oh, Granny," he answered, "I promise you—no one's food tastes as good as this."

"So, Albert, we just stay?" Papa asked.

"We just sit tight, brother. Nobody moves one inch. Mr. Lekota says the new church will be built, and he will be preaching in it to his congregation; *he* is not intending to move. If we all resist together, what can they do? But if a few families start to go, *then* they can come in and bulldoze a few empty houses. Then . . . *fear*. Then there will be a place for fear to spread. Then a few more will go, and a few more. . . . Then, *they* will have won, and the rest of us can start packing. . . ."

"It's more than our houses, Albert," Mama said. "It's our jobs as well."

"It's even more, sister. It's our *lives*. We have to show them that they *cannot* move us around like a herd of cattle that you chase from one place to another with a big stick."

John remained silent. Rebecca saw that his gaze never moved from Big Albert, that he was listening, hungrily, to every word he spoke.

"For me," Papa said, "the important thing is to have food for my family, and a roof over our heads."

"That's true, brother. But the other thing is also true."

THAT NIGHT Rebecca had no bad dreams. She woke only once. Betty, in her yellow nightgown, lay asleep beside her. In the dark she could hear Mama's and Papa's even breathing. John slept deeply. Big Albert's reassuring laughter echoed in her mind; she remembered how the sound of it close to her back felt as if a great train were rushing by. From the kitchen came the sound of Granny softly snoring and the comforting *tick-tock*, *tick-tock* of the clock on the sideboard.

6

AFTER BIG ALBERT KOSANE'S visit, Rebecca no longer thought that the great trucks or tractors she saw from the top of the *koppie*, coming slowly along the dirt road, must be bulldozers moving in to crush their houses. She knew people were working on their side. Even lawyers, Big Albert had said. But she still sometimes had bad dreams. Once she dreamed she had lost Betty and found her at last lying pressed flat into the mud on the soccer field.

Rebecca and Noni, playing together, never talked about Pofadderkloof, as if they had an unspoken agreement. Noni said only that her father and mother had promised to think about what Big Albert had told them.

The dry wintery velt turned green. Jacaranda blossoms appeared on the tree; a man with a small cart pulled by a donkey came around calling in a singsong voice, *"Ripe red watermelons, very sweet, very cheap"*; women sat on blankets spread out where the buses and *kombis* pulled in from town, selling roasted ears of corn. Many people wanted summer dresses, and in the afternoons the sound of Granny's sewing machine whirred away in the kitchen.

The days were hot and still, and talk about bulldozers and Pofadderkloof faded away. When Rebecca got two gold stars at school, for spelling and for sums, Granny was pleased with her and sewed two dresses for Betty, one of pink and white striped cotton and one of blue with tiny red flowers.

THEN, ONE MORNING after the summer break, the teacher, Miss Molefe, was taking register, calling their names out one by one to know who was in class. There were two children absent—the Baleka twins. "I hope they're not sick," Miss Molefe said. "They certainly were well and full of mischief yesterday."

A boy at the back of the room put up his hand and called out, "They're not sick, Miss. They've moved."

"Moved!" Miss Molefe exclaimed. "That's impossible. I would know if they're moving. They would have had to ask me to get them transfers from the principal."

"They *moved*, Miss. I saw them. They live next door to us. Early this morning while it was still dark I heard sounds. I looked out of the window and I saw them loading their furniture onto a truck. There were some policemen helping them. They're not the only ones. Two other families on our road went as well. Someone told my mother. They all went while it was dark so that no one would see. They didn't tell anyone they were going."

It was so quiet that the song of a bird whistling high up in the blue-gum trees sounded sweet and clear in the classroom.

"They've gone to Pofadderkloof, Miss," another boy called out.

"How do you know that?" the teacher asked sharply.

"That's what my father said," he answered.

There was that look on Miss Molefe's face, Rebecca saw, the look she knew on the faces of grown-ups when trouble came. Sitting at her desk with a freshly sharpened pencil and her neat copybook with gold stars pasted in it, she felt afraid.

"All right, children," the teacher said. "No more talking. Let's get on with our work. Open up your books and start copying down these sums from the blackboard."

ALL DAY Rebecca felt an ache of worry in her stomach. At supper that evening, she told Papa about the three families who had moved.

"They're not the only ones," John said. "There are others. A boy on our soccer team—Daniel—his family left last night, and his cousin's family also. The police were there."

Papa looked concerned. "How is this thing going

to work unless we're all in it together?" he asked plaintively.

"They move while it's dark because they're afraid for the neighbors to see them go," John said.

"You say there were police helping them?" Papa asked.

"Protecting them," John said. "In case anyone tried to prevent them from leaving."

Papa drummed his fingers on the table. He looked around the room as if he had lost something.

"Better get over to Big Albert's place as soon as you've eaten," Granny told him. "Find out what's going on."

REBECCA, with Betty beside her, leaned against the trunk of the jacaranda tree, reading, in the warm evening light, one of the books Mama had bought at the church sale. It was a storybook with pictures of animals dressed in clothes, cooking, playing with toys, sitting at a table eating food with plates and spoons; a mother animal bathed her children and put them to bed. There was nice furniture in the house, comfortable sofas, carpets, flowered curtains at the windows. The two animal children had their own bedroom, with two beds and toy shelves and a chest of drawers. Rebecca looked for a long time at the picture of the bathroom with its white, clean bathtub and sink, shiny taps with steaming water gushing out, fat cakes of soap that foamed and bubbled when the mother animal scrubbed the children. The father animal wore glasses and sat in an armchair reading the newspaper.

She read that the animals were bears. She had never seen a bear. Their coats looked so thick and furry that she thought most likely the *veld* would be too hot for them. Perhaps they lived where it snowed. She would ask Miss Molefe. Rebecca enjoyed reading about animals who talked like people. Granny only liked to read the Bible, but she knew many stories that she had been told by her own granny, long ago, when she was a child. The stories she told Rebecca and John were also about animals who could talk— hyenas and monkeys and lions and elephants who were brave or wise or deceitful. They had magic powers and could trick people, or help them, or teach them lessons so that they would know how to behave better. But they didn't wear clothes and live in houses with bathrooms and kitchens like the bears in the storybook.

Noni came by with a group of school friends. "We're going to have a skipping-rope competition. Are you coming, Rebecca?"

Rebecca's stomach still hurt a little. She shook her head. "I don't feel like skipping."

"I'll stay with you then," Noni said, and the others trooped off without her, laughing and arguing about who would turn the rope first.

Noni sat down under the tree. On the ground beside the doll's box were more books about the same bear family. She picked one up and leafed through it. "These animals are wearing clothes," she remarked. "Look at the nice party dress this one has on. I wouldn't mind a slice of that birthday cake." She rubbed her stomach. "We didn't have much for supper."

"Look what a nice bathroom they have in their house." Rebecca showed Noni the picture of the mother bear soaping her children in the gleaming white bathtub.

"Where did you get these books?" Noni asked.

"My mother bought them at a church sale."

"My auntie Miriam is going to buy me a coloring book and some crayons." Noni turned the page. "What kind of animals are these supposed to be?"

"It says here they are bears."

"Bears!" Noni wrinkled up her nose. "I've never heard of them. Can I hold Betty?"

Rebecca nodded and Noni took Betty out of the box. She straightened her dress, retied her sash, tipped her over to make her cry *Mama*, laid her back and sat her up to make her eyes open and close, then rocked her in her arms and sang a little African song to her. "She's asleep now. . . . Auntie Miriam knows another family who moved out today."

"I don't want to talk about it." Rebecca looked firmly at her book.

"She says now more and more people will be starting to go."

"We're not going," Rebecca said.

"Neither are we, now. Big Albert Kosane explained to my parents why we should stay. They agreed. But after he left, my mother started to argue with my father."

Rebecca looked up. "She *wants* to move?"

"Oh, no. She has too many cousins here, and friends. She doesn't want to leave them. But she says she really would like to have a bigger house. . . ."

Rebecca looked at her in stony silence.

"But my father says it's going to be too far for him to travel to work," Noni went on. "My auntie Miriam too—she has to be at the old people's home *very* early in the morning. She says she'd have to start out in the middle of the night to get to work on time."

"I told you I don't want to talk about it," Rebecca said. "My father's at a meeting at Big Albert's right now. I'm sick and tired of all the talk, talk, talk— moving—not moving—Pofadderkloof—bulldozers. It makes my stomach hurt."

"Let's change Betty's dress then," Noni said. "Can we put on the pink-and-white one?"

"All right. Look. My granny has sewed her a matching bonnet."

"REBECCA," Granny called from the doorway. "Come and do your homework while there's still some light. We're running out of kerosene for the lamp, and there won't be any more until your father gets paid on Friday."

After her homework was done Rebecca wanted to stay up for Papa, but Granny sent her to bed. Even though she didn't want to think about Pofadderkloof, she lay awake waiting for him to come home so that she could hear what Big Albert had decided they should do. She tried to keep her mind inside the house of the bear family—their kitchen with its scoured pots and pans, their living room with a piano, plump armchairs, pictures, vases of flowers, but her eyes grew heavy and she fell asleep.

At breakfast next morning, first thing, John asked Papa, "What did Big Albert say?"

"There's going to be a big gathering," Papa told them. "A march. A protest meeting—to save the village. We're going to go around to all the houses and ask everyone to join us. We're going to make it clear to this government that even though they have managed to scare a few families into leaving, the rest of us are staying here and *not budging.*"

"*Hau!*" With a can opener Granny popped a hole in the top of a can of sweetened condensed milk and poured some into a mug of tea for Rebecca. "We have enough trouble as it is. Why do they have to make life so hard for the black people?" She shook her head, tore a piece from a thick slice of white bread, dipped it into her tea, and ate it.

Rebecca stirred her tea, watching the thick white milk swirl into the dark liquid until it was clouded through. The tea was sweet and hot. She sipped it slowly while Papa spoke.

"There's a committee been formed: The Committee to Save the Village," Papa was telling John. "They need people to help with posters and placards. The office is at Big Albert's house. I told them you would go there straight after school, my boy."

"But I have soccer practice this afternoon, Papa."

Their father looked grave. "This is more important than soccer, Johnny."

"All right," John agreed. "I'll go. But my handwriting isn't so good, Papa."

"I think what they want you for is to go around the village putting up posters and notices about the demonstration."

John looked pleased. "I'd like to do that," he said.

7

"HURRY UP, REBECCA," Granny said, a few days later. "Look at the time. You'll be late for school."

Papa had left for work and John had gone in early to school to get extra help with his arithmetic.

"The clock must be fast," Rebecca said, turning the page of one of her bear books. "I'm waiting for Noni. She's always on time—so the clock must be wrong."

"The clock is right, my child. Noni's late, and she'll make you late. Take your books and go and get her." Granny hustled her out of the house.

Rebecca hated to be late, particularly on Monday, when the teacher read them a story before lessons began. "Bye, Granny." She hurried out past the jacaranda tree and through the gate, and turned into Noni's front yard. Halfway down the path, she stopped. Her heart turned over in her chest and began to thump heavily. She felt her mouth go dry. Her schoolbag clutched in her hand, she stood unmoving, one foot in front of the other, as if she had been turned into a piece of wood.

In the bright sunshine, the front door of Noni's house was shut fast. Curtainless windows stared at Rebecca. No sound came from inside—no wailing and howling babies, no shouts and cries of the little brothers. Only silence, and emptiness.

Slowly Rebecca stirred herself to move. She approached the house. She peered in through a window. The living room was bare except for a couple of empty kerosene tins, a chair with a leg missing, a bright green plastic toy truck, broken and abandoned in a corner.

Feet dragging, Rebecca turned and walked away. She wanted to go home and lie facedown on the bed, not talk to anyone, not see anyone. But she knew Granny wouldn't allow it. She knew she should go back and tell Granny, but she walked on, past her own house, along the dusty red dirt road to school.

Though it was still early, the sun was already burning as though it wanted to shrivel up everything in its path. It felt strange to be walking to school without Noni. They had started school together on their very first day; Noni called for her every morning; they always walked together and sat near each other in class—and walked home together every afternoon.

Some girls ran by, calling out to her, but Rebecca

didn't hear what they said, didn't answer. She felt a tight, dry lump in her throat, but no tears came. She walked on toward the school building, knowing that the teacher would ask her where Noni was, knowing what her answer would have to be. She could see the children lining up in front of the classrooms, some latecomers hurrying across the school yard. She heard the school bell ring, but, as though overtaken by a bad dream in the bright daylight, was unable to walk any faster.

In the afternoon, when the girls came by to fetch her to play, Rebecca shook her head and they went off without her. She sat under the jacaranda tree so that her back was turned to Noni's house. Without the bustle of family life—playthings strewn everywhere, the noisy little boys rolling about in the dust laughing, quarreling, their auntie Miriam with her beads and bangles and loud laugh, the sound of their overworked mother's voice scolding, calling, the bright curtains in the window—the place was a small, deserted hovel. She couldn't bear to face it now.

Along with the bear books, Mama had bought at the church sale a toffee tin filled with crayons, and a big coloring book. The crayons were mostly broken, but Rebecca found she could use the bigger pieces quite easily if she peeled away some of the paper covering. The book was thick and only a few of the pictures had been filled in, so there were plenty of them for her to work on. Very carefully, pressing hard so that the colors would come bright and clear, she completed a picture of a boy and girl walking in a forest of tall trees. The boy had a piece of bread in his hand and was crumbling it and strewing it on the ground as he went. He had left a trail of crumbs on the path behind them. She wondered if he was leaving food for the birds who were watching from the tree branches. She thought it must be cool and shady in a place with so many trees. There weren't many in the village; if she looked down from the *koppie* when the jacaranda was in bloom, the blue-mauve of its flowers was the only splash of color among the drab houses and the thornbushes and the yellow-brown of the *veld*. She chose a crayon the color of the jacaranda blossoms to fill in a clump of flowers growing alongside the forest path.

The gate opened and John came into the yard. He looked pleased and important. "Eddie Maboko and I pasted up fifteen posters about the demonstration," he announced.

Rebecca chose another crayon from the tin and went on with her coloring.

"Oh, you're not interested," John grumbled, and went inside.

Rebecca gathered up her things and followed her brother into the house. She sat down at the kitchen table and took out her schoolbooks.

At the stove Granny was stirring the *putu* and

muttering to herself. "After all these years . . ." she was saying, "all these years we've been next-door neighbors. . . . How many times have I helped them when the little ones were sick? . . . And when he lost his job that time, and their bag of *mealie meal* was empty and we could hear the little ones crying from hunger, didn't we give them food? . . . Didn't I sew clothes for them? . . . And Miriam—telling me her troubles with her boyfriends and asking my advice and bringing me dress patterns to sew her the latest fashion. . . . And now, like jackals in the night they sneak off—they go—without a word to any of us. . . . *Gone*. What is happening? . . . What is happening to this world when people start to do things like this?"

"Gone!" John exclaimed. "The Mkwanes?" He turned to Rebecca. "Noni's gone?"

Her throat tightened and no words came. She nodded.

John came and stood beside Rebecca's chair. "I'm sorry for you, little sister," he said. He turned to Granny. "I came home the other way. I didn't notice they weren't there. They must have gone in the middle of the night."

"In the dark, like jackals," Granny intoned.

Rebecca opened her book to a clean page and began to write out her six-times tables. If she kept her mind on her multiplication she didn't hear what John and Granny were saying.

When Papa's *kombi* dropped him off she didn't run

to greet him as she always did. She worked away at her arithmetic not even looking up to say hello. He and Granny spoke for a little, then he came and sat beside her and lifted her onto his lap. He rested his chin gently on her head. "Your little friend Noni is gone, my child," he said in a sad voice. "I am sorry for you."

She wriggled off his lap. "I have to finish my homework, Papa."

She saw Papa give Granny a look. Granny went back to stirring the *putu*, her spoon banging angrily against the pot. Moving slowly, heavily, Papa went into the bedroom to change out of his work clothes. John came in lugging a bucket of water Granny had sent him to fetch. Bursting to tell Papa about the work he had done for Big Albert's committee, he plonked the bucket down and went into the bedroom. Through the door Rebecca heard their voices, John eager, pleased with himself; Papa questioning, interested, praising.

8

ON TUESDAY EVENING at supper, Papa said, "Mama phoned me today at work. She won't be coming home on Thursday. She has a toothache and has to go to the dentist."

"Why must she go on her day off?" John complained. "And she's not off this Sunday either. Now I have to wait nearly two weeks to tell her about Big Albert's committee. What's the matter with those white people! Can't they even give her a couple of hours off to go to the dentist?"

"They don't think that way," Granny said. "I know them. I worked in the houses of white people from the time I was seventeen. They only know how to think about what suits them."

Nearly two weeks before Mama would be home again. . . . There was not much gravy tonight and the *putu* was hard to swallow. Rebecca pushed her food away.

Papa was watching her. "No need to look so

sad my girlie." He patted her shoulder. "I have a treat for you. I've asked for the day off on Saturday. And I'm taking you and John to visit Mama in town."

"We're going to visit her! In the *kombi* . . ."

Papa laughed. "That's right, my child. To visit Mama. In the *kombi*."

"But Papa," John wailed, "I'm supposed to go to a meeting at Big Albert's on Saturday."

"Very well, John. We'll tell Mama how busy and important you're becoming."

"But it's not fair," John grumbled.

"Tell them you can't come to the meeting, then, and come with us."

"I can't do that," John said. "I have to go to Big Albert's."

"Then that's that," Papa said.

"Good boy, Johnny," Granny remarked, and John looked pleased because she seldom gave compliments.

"Can I bring Betty?" Rebecca asked Papa.

"Betty? Who's that?"

"Betty's her dolly," John explained. "She wants to take her dolly," he teased, and would have gone on teasing if Granny hadn't tweaked his ear.

"Of course!" Papa laughed. "I don't think they'll charge extra for her on the *kombi*."

"Eat up your food, child," Granny told her.

Rebecca felt hungry again. She took back her plate, and soon it was empty and she was full.

AFTER SCHOOL on Thursday, when Mama would have been home, Rebecca went with some other girls to the top of the *koppie*. But without Noni it wasn't the same, and she came back on her own after a while and played with Betty. It seemed to her that Betty was also missing Noni; so she put her to sleep in her box and sat down under the jacaranda tree to read the bear books instead.

Thoughts of the visit to Mama kept getting in the way of the bears. The book lay open on her lap as she recalled her last visit. She remembered a little white girl and a green garden filled with flowers. It was a long time ago, when she was much younger; but she still clearly remembered the excitement of the bus ride—it was in the days before the *kombis* started to run. She remembered the stretch of farmland they drove through, with cows grazing, the silver blades of windmills turning against the blue air. And the sudden way, as they approached the town, that the sea came swinging into view. One moment there was nothing but farms and *veld*, and then—there it was. The sea. It lay so huge and quiet, stretching all the way out until it met the sky, all that water, always there, even when she couldn't see it, as if it was waiting, always waiting.

ON SATURDAY morning Rebecca was up early. She dressed Betty in her matching dress and bonnet.

After she'd been out to the tap to wash, she put on the clothes Granny had washed and ironed for her—a pink T-shirt and a yellow-and-pink flowered skirt Granny had sewn from a piece of fabric left over from a dress she'd once made for Noni's auntie Miriam. Granny had cleaned her sandals with whitener from a tube so that they looked brand-new. From a drawer Rebecca took out a brass bangle with coils of tiny colored beads worked into it. She slipped it onto her wrist and tried to see how she looked in the mirror on the chest of drawers. But it was too small and she could see only bits of her reflection at a time.

She was too excited to eat much breakfast, impatient to be walking hand in hand with Papa to the *kombi*. In the doorway, Granny and John waved goodbye. Rebecca had got into the habit of averting her eyes whenever she passed by Noni's sad and empty house, and she turned her head now to watch some boys chasing about on the soccer field.

They were early and able to get seats on the side of the *kombi* from which the sea would come into view. She held Betty firmly on her lap. Soon all the seats were taken and the *kombi* rumbled off. An early morning fog had rolled in from the coast, hiding everything under a gray blanket of damp. Rebecca was disappointed that there was nothing to see but gray shapes beyond the window; but as they drove along the sun climbed the sky, burning off the mist. The countryside began to appear at last, the gray

54

shapes turning into a group of thatched huts here, a herd of cows drinking at a dam there, a woman walking barefoot across the *veld* with a baby tied in a blanket on her back. Then, many miles on, suddenly, something shimmering far off, blue and flat, a long line against the sky.

"The sea! Look, Papa—the sea—the sea!" She shook Papa's arm, but he was busy talking across the aisle to a man he knew. She supposed that since he came this way every day, traveling to and from work, the sight of the sea wasn't as exciting to him.

As they drew closer to the coast she saw boats, looking no bigger than her hand, bobbing on the great blue sheet of water wrinkled, she could see now, with small waves that glittered as they caught the sunlight. She held Betty up to the window. "Look, Betty, look at the sea," she whispered, "the sea." Flocks of gulls were hovering, wheeling and swooping above the fishing boats. Through the open windows came the high, mewing sound of their cries. Watching them, Rebecca remembered the smell of the ocean. She had been taken to the beach once, a few years ago, on a church outing. She still recalled the sugary feel of the fine white sand under her bare feet, between her toes, the salt smell of the breeze, the great boom of the waves rising up in curves of green water before they crashed down on the beach to push along foam as white as boiling milk. Some of the children had bathed, but she had been glad not to have had a swimsuit, as the din and hugeness of the breakers between the jagged rocks had scared her. She'd paddled at the edge of the water, she and Noni, the two of them laughing and running screaming away when the water rushed at them to swirl fast and deep around their legs. They had made sand-cakes by letting the wet sand drip through their fingers until it piled up in strange shapes. They had been given slices of watermelon and had washed the sweet stickiness off their hands in the cold salt water.

The beach they'd been taken to was reserved for black bathers. Further along, separated by coils of barbed wire, was the whites' beach; they saw the pale sand dotted with bright colors of bathing suits, gaily striped umbrellas, and canvas chairs. There were no rocks. White children with buckets and spades were playing, eating ice-cream cones, splashing unafraid in the waves that broke along the water's edge. The few black people on the other beach were nursemaids. They were taking care of white children whose parents lay baking in the sun or swimming where the water was deep. The salt-smelling breeze had carried to her the sound of the white children's shouts and laughter.

"Papa." She shook his arm now to get his attention.

"What is it, Rebecca?"

"Papa. Will you take us to the beach one day?"

"You need to have a car to get to the beach, child."

"Couldn't we go in the *kombi*?"

"Yes. But the *kombi* costs money; if we used it whenever we wanted, then there wouldn't be enough left to buy *putu* for your supper." He resumed the conversation with his friend. Rebecca heard the word Pofadderkloof. She looked determinedly out of the window, thinking about that day at the beach.

Soon they were passing small houses with flower-filled gardens on the outskirts of the town, then they were slowed by heavy traffic crowding the main highway, the *kombi* crawling like a tortoise in an endless stream of cars, buses, trucks, and vans. The slowness didn't bother Rebecca; every bit of the trip was exciting to her. She enjoyed looking at the people in the passing cars. Nearly all were white. An old man with no hair and a funny round nose like a blob of red clay seemed to be having an argument with his wife, whose head was thatched, like a hut, with bright yellow hair; her scarf and lipstick were the same shade of purple as one of Rebecca's crayons. In the back of another car she saw a black nursemaid feeding a baby with a bottle, while the baby's mother and father seemed almost to be dancing in the front seat to music blaring out of the windows. Rebecca noticed the way rays of sunshine inside the cars lit up the ears of the white men so that the rims glowed bright pink. She thought, *I must tell Noni how funny their ears look.* Then she remembered about Noni, and the bad feeling she had been trying to keep back welled up and stayed with her until the *kombi* stopped and the doors opened to let them out.

THE CENTER of town was thronged with traffic and Saturday morning shoppers, black and white. Holding tightly onto Betty, Rebecca slipped her hand into Papa's and they made their way to the bus stop. She looked with curiosity at the white people hurrying along the sidewalks and in and out of shops. Few whites ever came to the village—policemen, sometimes government inspectors, a nurse and doctor occasionally to give shots at the clinic. The white women in the town were dressed in pretty, light-colored clothes; their arms were bare, and pink really, rather than white, and they wore lots of jewelry.

The bus they had to take to the suburb where Mama worked was waiting at the terminus, and soon they were on their way again. Rebecca was beginning to feel hungry and wished she had eaten her breakfast.

The bus was for black people only. The whites used other buses. She sat silent beside Papa, Betty cradled in her arms, watching out of the window. After the dry, yellow-brown of the *veld*, the sight of the green gardens of the suburbs—lawns, trees, flowers—was like a cool drink of water on a hot day. The houses were of golden brick, or painted pink, pale yellow, white. She could see the blue water of swimming pools in many of the gardens, and even the sidewalks were planted with mowed grass; flowers and cactuses and shrubs grew along the outsides of the high garden walls. Most of the houses had tall iron gates as well. Through them there was no one to be seen, apart from black gardeners at work, and, here and there, women like Mama who were house servants. Rebecca wondered where all the white people were, why they remained hidden behind their high walls.

She noticed printed signs on many of the gates, and when the bus stopped at a busy crossroad, she was able to read one of them. *"Ace Security System,"* she read out aloud. *"Immediate armed guard response* . . . What does that mean, Papa?" she asked.

"Oh—these white people are all afraid. So if someone who shouldn't be there tries to get in, a loud siren goes off, and straightaway a car arrives with guards and guns and dogs."

"What are they afraid of, Papa?"

"They're afraid of what is coming to them one day."

"What is coming to them?"

"Oh—" he patted her—"don't you worry about these things, my child."

"I'm thirsty, Papa."

"We're nearly there. Your mother will give you something to drink."

"If I had one of those houses, I wouldn't sit inside."

"What would you do, little one?"

"I'd sit out on the grass with Betty, under a shady

tree, and look at the flowers, and drink a bottle of orange soda through a straw."

He laughed. "You'll be able to do that soon. We're nearly there. Mama will give you a nice cold drink. She told me there's a birthday party for one of the children this afternoon. She'll be busy. But she'll have some time off after lunch. You'll be able to play and look at flowers all you want. Here's our stop now. Come along."

9

THE GATE BETWEEN the stone pillars had a row of sharp spikes along the top. Rebecca could see no way of opening it. "How will we get in, Papa?" she asked.

"Watch what happens," he told her. In one of the pillars there was a button set under a small brass grille. Papa pressed the button. There was a crackling sound and suddenly, from somewhere inside the gatepost, a man's voice boomed out, "Who is it?"

The voice, coming from nowhere, so startled Rebecca that she backed away nervously, grabbing Papa's sleeve.

"It's me, Amos—Martha's husband—and the child," Papa said to the gatepost.

"Oh, hi, Amos, I'll buzz you in."

To Rebecca's astonishment the gate began to slide away sideways, silently gliding open until there was space enough for them to walk through. Then, as though held by an unseen hand, it stopped.

"Come along," Papa said, but she held back, afraid it might start to close on them as they passed.

"Come along!" Papa took her by the hand, and as soon as they had stepped beyond it, the gate shut behind them. They were locked in.

"How will we get out?" she whispered.

"Don't worry, child. It will be all right."

When she had been here before, that time many years ago, she remembered she had walked through an ordinary gate that swung open and clicked shut like the one in the front yard at home. "This is a new kind of gate, Papa. Is it magic?"

He laughed. "It's electric."

A brick path set in a lawn bordered by flowers led to the front door of the house, but Papa led Rebecca around the back, past the garage, into a paved yard. The back door stood open and just as Papa was about to rap on it with his knuckles, Mama appeared in the doorway. "Here you are," she said with a broad smile.

Rebecca had been missing her mother for so long; she ran forward to hug her and be hugged and hardly wanted to let go to let her greet Papa. Mama was dressed in a pink uniform, starched and crisply ironed, with a matching pink kerchief tied over her hair. Her eyes were bright with the pleasure of seeing them, and her smiling cheeks, smooth and plump, glowed as if they had been polished. "You look so pretty, Mama," Rebecca said, "like a nurse."

Mama and Papa laughed. "Oh, my madam likes us to wear pink overalls. It's lucky I like pink."

"I brought Betty."

"I see. And Granny has made her some new clothes."

"The child is thirsty," Papa said.

"What would you like to drink, little one?"

"An orange soda."

REBECCA sat on the back doorstep, her doll propped up beside her, sipping the cold orange soda through a straw while Mama and Papa talked and laughed in the kitchen. A buttery smell of baking filled the air.

"So, this is Rebecca." She heard a voice behind her and stood up. In the kitchen Mama's madam had appeared. She was a tall woman in white shorts and a bright green blouse. She was barefoot. Her hair was black and cut close to her head like a man's, and long white earrings dangled above her shoulders. "You were quite little the last time I saw you," she said. "How old are you now, Rebecca?"

"Nine," she said shyly.

"That's right. I remember now—same age as Mandy. Today's her ninth birthday."

"Mandy is much bigger than Rebecca, Ma'm," Mama said.

"You must eat all your *putu*, Rebecca," Madam said, "so you can grow big and strong. Martha—"

she turned to Mama—"have you iced the cupcakes yet?"

"Yes, Ma'm. They're in the pantry."

"And the jellies?"

"In the fridge."

"What about the sandwiches?"

"I'll do them after lunch, Ma'm. If I do them too early they dry out."

"Fine." She turned to Papa. "You're looking well, Amos."

"I'm very well thank you, Ma'm."

"Fine!" Madam looked vaguely around the kitchen and wandered out.

Rebecca crossed the threshold and put the empty bottle down on the sink near the back door. Mama was making tea for Papa. When she rinsed the teapot under the tap, steaming hot water came gushing out just like in the kitchen in the bear book. But this kitchen was far grander than the bears', and everything in it was white.

Rebecca heard a cry and a small boy came staggering toward her on fat legs, followed by a nursemaid dressed in a pink uniform and kerchief just like Mama's. The baby sat down on the floor and banged a rubber toy on Papa's shoe, making them all laugh. The nursemaid greeted them, chattering away while she lifted the baby into a high chair and sat down to feed him some mashed food.

"Come and see the baby, Rebecca," Mama said.

But Rebecca felt shy and hung back. "Would you like to go and play in the garden?" Mama suggested.

Rebecca nodded. "I'll take Betty," she said. She went out and found a path leading around the side of the house into the garden. The day was hot. On the lawn a sprinkler was whirling sprays of water, soaking the grass. Rebecca took off her sandals and stepped barefoot onto the cool, soft, damp green. Bees hummed in the flowerbeds and in the trees birds twittered and sang. The gardener, an old black man with grizzled silver hair, was on his knees weeding between the flowers. He was friendly and asked her how old she was and what grade she was in at school.

"Go and enjoy the flowers, my child," he told her, "and help yourself to the figs on that tree. *They* never eat them and they are all going to waste. Feel them—if they are nice and soft, it means they are ripe."

The tree was bowed low under the weight of its fruit. No one had been picking the figs and many of them, overripe, had burst open, exposing vivid pink insides. Figs that had fallen to the ground gave off a sweet, rotten smell; ants crawled over them, busily feasting. Rebecca watched as a small yellow bird settled on a branch and started to peck at the center of a burst fruit; it was a pretty sight—the bright yellow of the bird beside the pink fig among the glossy green, broad fig leaves.

Someone spoke suddenly. "Are you Rebecca?"

With a flutter of yellow wings the bird flew off.

Rebecca turned. A white girl had come up behind her. "Yes," she answered.

"I wondered whose sandals those were." The girl stared at her with curiosity. "I remember you. You were here once, a long time ago. We were both little."

Rebecca remained silent. The girl's hair was cut short, black and shiny like her mother's. She was thin and tall and looked just like the madam, Rebecca thought. She remembered her from that last visit; she had been small and plump then, with her hair in pigtails. She was wearing a swimsuit and carrying a wet towel. "I've just come from my swimming lesson," she said. "Can you swim?"

Rebecca shook her head.

"Today's my birthday. I'm nine."

"I'm also nine," Rebecca said.

The girl wrinkled up her nose. "I hate the smell of those rotten figs. Do you like figs?"

Rebecca shrugged.

The girl noticed Betty in Rebecca's hand. "That used to be *my* doll. Her name is Lulu."

Rebecca clutched the doll tightly. "It's not. It's Betty."

"Where did you get those clothes for her?"

"My granny made them."

The girl turned and walked away. Rebecca watched her cross the lawn to a broad veranda and disappear through a sliding glass door into the house. She looked at Betty, retied the strings of her bonnet, and straightened out her dress. "You're *not* Lulu," she said to the doll. "You're Betty."

In the tree the yellow bird had settled on another branch and was feeding again at a fig. Rebecca decided to taste one. She plucked it and the fig came away leaving a milky drop at the end of the stem. She split it open; the soft sticky interior was flecked with tiny seeds. She licked it with the tip of her tongue. It was sweet and syrupy, but when she bit and chewed a piece the fuzzy skin was rough and unpleasant on her tongue, so she dropped it under the tree for the birds and the ants, put on her sandals, and went back to the kitchen.

AFTER MAMA had served lunch to the white people, Rebecca and Mama and Papa had a meal together in Mama's room. It was a small, neat room with a high narrow bed and a table and chair and cupboard. There were three servants' rooms attached to the garage: one for Mama, one for the nursemaid, and one for the gardener. There was a small bathroom with a shower, and a stove where the servants did their own cooking. Mama had prepared a big pot of *putu* and meat, and Rebecca ate until her stomach was tight and full. Then Mama brought a dish of figs. "I don't like figs," Rebecca said. "I tasted one in the garden and it made my tongue feel funny."

"You're supposed to peel them, silly one," Mama told her. "Here, taste this without the skin."

Rebecca tried the fruit. "It's sweet, like jam," she said.

"If we don't eat them they just go to waste. They let them rot on the tree. Madam wants me to make fig jam—but they keep me so busy I don't have the time. Here, I've peeled another one for you."

"No more, thank you, Mama." The taste of the fig made her remember the girl in the garden saying her doll's name was Lulu. . . .

After they had drunk tea, Papa lay down on the bed for a nap. The afternoon was still and hot. In the trees the cooing of the doves made a peaceful, drowsy sound. Mama sat at the table crocheting a hat.

"Mama," Rebecca said.

"What is it, my child?"

"Mama—did Papa tell you . . . ?"

"Tell me what?"

"Tell you—that Noni—" She swallowed, unable to finish her sentence. She felt the tears rising up in her and burst out crying; she went and laid her head on her mother's lap, and cried and cried.

"Oh, my little one . . ." Mama patted her, stroked her. "Oh little one, I know, I know. . . . Papa told me. I wanted to talk to you about it but you were having a happy day and I didn't want to spoil it. How hard it is for you—your best friend. You played together since you were babies . . . I know . . . I know . . ."

"And she didn't even tell me they were going," Rebecca sobbed. "She didn't come and fetch me to go to school on Monday. . . . And I went—I went next door—and the house was *empty*. . . ." Against Mama's lap her body was racked with weeping, with shuddering sobs.

"Shh . . . little one, shh . . ."

"The house was empty and they were all *gone*. . . . She was my best friend and she didn't even tell me . . . and now—and now—" Mama's apron grew damp with Rebecca's tears. "And now—I have no one to play with."

Mama lifted Rebecca onto her lap and wiped her eyes and face with the corner of her apron. "Don't be cross with Noni, my dear," she said. "I know she wanted to tell you. But you can be sure that her parents had forbidden her to whisper even a word about it to *anyone*. Those people from the planning department—when they've persuaded someone to leave, they warn them not to tell anybody at all. Not even their close relatives. Think how hard it must have been also for Noni—to know she was leaving the village and not be allowed to tell even her best friend. Don't be cross with Noni, Rebecca. We have to feel sorrow for her—poor child—who will *she* play with in—in *that place*. You still have your school friends."

Thinking now of Noni's loneliness made Rebecca cry harder. "Why did they have to go there?" she wept. *"We're* staying. Why couldn't they? Oh, why don't they let us stay where we are, Mama? *Why* do they want to come and bulldoze our houses? Why can't they just leave us alone?" The tears she had been storing all week fell now like salt rain, her body shaking as the sorrow in her rose up, turned into words.

With a corner of her apron, Mama was dabbing her own eyes, holding onto Rebecca, rocking her and making soothing sounds like the cooing of the doves in the trees. In the stillness of the sun-filled afternoon, Papa, in his sleep, breathed a long, shuddering sigh as if he was having a bad dream. Mama held her, rocking to and fro.

MAMA dabbed Rebecca's eyes and nose with a hankie and sent her to wash her face. The handfuls of cold water that gushed from the tap splashed away the dried saltiness of the tears that prickled her cheeks, and cooled her burning eyes. She went into the kitchen and sat at the table watching as Mama made tiny, crustless sandwiches; following her about as she set the dining-room table for the birthday party.

Beyond the dining room, the living room looked to Rebecca as big as the church hall in the village. She stared in wonder at the white sofas and easy chairs, the low glass tables holding ornaments and great vases of garden flowers, the soft carpets, the pictures on the walls.

Mama set out on the table red and yellow jellies in cups made of hollowed-out orange halves, cakes, cookies, candies, nuts and raisins, sandwiches, bottles of colored sodas. In the center she placed a white iced birthday cake with nine pink candles on it. It was even better than the bears' cake in the book.

"You made that cake all by yourself, Mama?"

"I did. All by myself."

"All those pink icing roses?"

Mama laughed. "It's not hard to do, Rebecca. Those pink roses—I just squeeze the icing through a special tube my madam has, and out they come like that."

"Mama, you're so clever."

"Martha!" The white girl came into the dining room. "*Martha*. Why did *you* put the candles on the cake. It's not fair . . . I *told* you I wanted to do it myself." She looked very cross. She was dressed in a pretty blue-flowered dress that reached to her ankles and shiny white shoes, and she had a blue bow clipped in her hair.

"Sorry, Mandy. I forgot. I wanted everything to be in place," Mama answered.

"Well, you *shouldn't* have! And you haven't made any green jellies," she complained. "You *know* lime is my favorite."

"Your mother only bought red and yellow—so you must be satisfied with what there is."

Rebecca saw a strange expression come over the girl's face. It looked like a smile, but underneath there was something else. "Martha—" she held out her forefinger and curled it over the birthday cake— "what would you do if I scooped up this pink rose in the middle, and gobbled it up?"

"It's your cake," Mama said. "If you want to ruin it, go ahead." Tray in hand, she left the room, followed by Rebecca.

Once they were in the kitchen, Rebecca asked, "Why would she want to do that—spoil her own cake!"

"She's only showing off," Mama said. "She's a spoiled child. The madam and the master, they both spoil her."

Rebecca knew what a spoiled cake was. She wondered how a child could be spoiled.

MAMA brought some books from the shelves in the playroom, and Rebecca settled down to read at the kitchen table. Papa sat outside in the sunshine in the backyard, chatting with the gardener. Children were arriving for the party. Rebecca could hear them shouting and laughing on the front lawn. Mama was busy. Madam, looking flurried, went in and out of the kitchen. "Reading, Rebecca? Fine, fine." She seemed to be talking to herself and took no more notice of Rebecca after that.

When the children were seated around the table for the birthday tea, Rebecca went and stood in the doorway to watch. She counted ten children, as well as Mandy's five-year-old brother and the baby in his high chair with the nanny beside him. The nanny beckoned to Rebecca, drawing her into the room and putting her arm around her. A few mothers stood about the table. One of them smiled at Rebecca in a friendly way. The children all looked at her, but no one said anything to her.

There was a lot of noise and chatter. Rebecca wished Noni could see the pretty frocks the girls were wearing. The five-year-old brother had a temper tantrum and was carried off, yelling and kicking, by a lady the nanny said was their auntie. Rebecca noticed that the children didn't eat much—a spoonful or so of jelly, a bite out of a sandwich. One of the mothers gave Rebecca an iced cupcake covered with tiny colored balls; it grew warm and sticky in her hand, as she felt too shy to eat it there. The woman also offered her a bottle of red soda, which Rebecca sucked up slowly through a straw.

"Where is the father of the children?" she whispered to the nanny.

"Oh, he's gone to play golf," she said. "He says he can't stand the noise."

The candles were lit and blown out. Everyone sang "Happy Birthday" and "For She's a Jolly Good Fellow," while Mandy, her cheeks red, scowled down at the tablecloth. The cake was cut and served.

"What about some birthday cake for Rebecca?" Madam said in a loud voice. Everyone stared at Rebecca, who remained silent.

"She'll have some later, Ma'm," the nanny answered for her.

Just then the little brother came running in shouting, "The magician's here—the magician's here!"

Mandy jumped up from her chair and ran out, followed by all the guests. The table was left littered with paper napkins and uneaten food.

"Magician? What's that?" Rebecca asked the nanny.

"Come, child. You'll see. He does tricks." She lifted the baby out of the high chair. "Come with me."

✎ OUT ON the lawn the children were all seated around a man with thick, curly red hair; he was very thin and had a pale, sad, funny face.

"He's the magician. Sit down here beside me," the nanny told her. Rebecca sat on the veranda step next to the baby, who wanted to play with the beads of her bangle and laughed and tried to grab it when she twirled it around her wrist for him.

The magician rattled two sticks on a tiny drum and everyone fell quiet. Then, to Rebecca's astonishment, fluttering and moving his long thin fingers so quickly that his hands seemed to fly about on their own, he made objects disappear before the children's eyes, pulled handkerchiefs out of people's ears, jerked

74

a toy rabbit out of an empty hat, put a scarf in his left ear and pulled it out of his right. Colored balls appeared from nowhere, colored rings spun in the air, bright scarves flowed out of a matchbox. He showed them a red strip of paper, shook it, and it turned into a flock of paper birds; he filled his mouth full of small plastic balls and pulled them out all strung together into a necklace.

On the veranda step Rebecca sat entranced, her eyes round with wonder.

"And now, kiddies," the magician said, "can you all see? I have in my hand this small green frog." He walked around, stooping low, flinging his gangling legs about in a comical way that made them all laugh, showing them the small frog carved out of green stone. He came up to Rebecca, showed her the frog, then stepped back into the circle of children. "Right. Now. Can you all see it—here in the palm of my hand?"

"Yes!" the children shouted, Rebecca as well.

"Well now, kiddies, this is a *magic* frog. Watch closely now . . . Everybody watching? . . . Shh . . . I want absolute silence while I say the magic words." His fingers closed around the frog.

There was silence. Even the baby stayed quiet.

"*Abra—kadabra kabobble—kadoodle ka-froggle—ka-froogle.*" He flung his hand open. It was empty! The frog had disappeared. The children gasped in surprise.

"Hmm . . . that's funny. Where could that froggy

little friend of mine have got to, I wonder? . . .
Anyone know where he is? Anyone got him?"

"*No!*" the children chorused.

"Hmm . . . I wonder . . ." The magician
scratched the top of his head. "Let me see now . . ."
He walked over to the veranda step. "Oho!" he said
to Rebecca. "What's *your* name, little girl?" he asked,
his smile forming deep creases in his thin cheeks.

She saw that his skin was covered with faint golden
freckles. She didn't feel at all shy of him. "Rebecca,"
she told him.

"Rebecca, that's a pretty name. Tell me, Rebecca
—do *you* know where my frog could have gone?"

Smiling, she shook her head. All the children had
turned to watch.

"Look in your pocket," he said.

She still held the cupcake in one hand. With the
other she reached into the pocket in the front of her
skirt. There was something in it. Something small
and hard. She couldn't believe it. She brought it out.
It was the frog! All the children cheered.

"How did it get in my pocket?" she asked.

"Magic," he said, taking the frog from her. He
touched Rebecca under her chin and smiled at her.

WHEN the magician's performance was over he
packed his magic tricks into a strapped canvas bag
and slung it across his back; then he climbed onto a
motorbike and waved good-bye to the children. Re-

76

becca stood waving as he roared away down the drive and out through the magic gate which slid open just long enough to allow him to pass through. Beyond the wall, she heard the growl of his engine grow fainter and fade away.

As soon as he left, the children crowded onto the veranda, where the birthday presents in colored wrappings were piled onto a table. Standing beside the nanny and the baby at the edge of the group, Rebecca watched as Mandy tore off the ribbons and ripped the pretty papers open to inspect each gift for a moment before turning to the next. The baby stretched out his fat arms wanting to grab dolls and books and games and sets of dollhouse furniture and tea sets and pots and pans. Many of the presents were in boxes, and Rebecca couldn't make out what they were. Once everything was opened, Mandy no longer seemed interested in her presents, and she and her friends trooped indoors to watch television.

"You can go with them if you like," the nanny said. "They're going to watch a children's film."

"I don't want to, thank you," Rebecca answered. She helped gather up the torn and crumpled wrappings. "Are you going to throw all this away?" she asked.

"Into the rubbish bin. This paper is expensive. They throw their money away." She removed a piece of blue paper the baby was chewing. "Look what you've done, you silly boy; now your face is all blue."

He looked as if he were about to start crying, but Rebecca gave him a bright yellow rosette to play with and he burst into smiles.

"Can I have some of the ribbons?" she asked.

"You can have them all, child."

Rebecca rolled up the prettiest ribbons and gathered a handful of rosettes—gold, silver, pink, purple. She thought, *I'll share these with Noni*; then, with a pang, she remembered about Noni.

"Go to the kitchen and ask your mother for a bag to put them in," the nanny told her.

WHILE Papa helped Mama wash up the dishes from the party, Rebecca sat at the kitchen table drinking tea and eating some of the party leftovers. She told them about the magic the magician had performed. "I really liked that man," she said. The iced cupcake, a little squashed, was on the table beside her.

"Why don't you eat it?" Mama asked.

"I'm saving it for John."

"Oh, don't worry about that. I'm packing a boxful of cakes and sandwiches for you to take home. Madam said I should. It will all go stale otherwise and I'll have to throw it out."

Rebecca peeled the paper off the cake. She bit through the crunchy sugared balls and sweet buttery icing, into the crumbly yellow cake. Papa was telling Mama how good it made John feel to be working for

Albert's committee to save the village. "He's busy now, every day, instead of being angry all the time."

"When are they holding the protest meeting?" Mama wanted to know.

"The last Sunday of the month."

"Good. That's my Sunday off. I want to be there in case there's trouble."

The excitement of the day, the party, the magician doing his magic in the green, beautiful garden, the safe feeling of being with Mama and Papa, the plentiful food, had pushed away worries about bulldozers. Now, swallowing the last of her cupcake as Mama and Papa spoke, she felt the ache of anxiety starting up again in her stomach. "What trouble will there be, Mama?"

"Don't worry about it, child. We'll take care of you."

Mama's voice was reassuring. Rebecca had cried so much after lunch that she was left feeling emptied out, without a place even to put her worry. "John will be sorry he missed the magician," she said.

"Finish your tea, child," Papa told her. "We must get back into town before the *kombi* leaves without us."

They said good-bye to Mama in the kitchen so she could buzz them out when they reached the gate. Mama hugged Rebecca tight. "Thursday's not many days off, little one. We'll be together soon."

Hand in hand with Papa she walked along the

path, Betty firmly under her arm and the box of party leftovers in a plastic bag dangling from her wrist. Papa carried a large shopping bag filled with food Mama had cooked for them. As they approached the gate it slid silently open, closing behind them as soon as they stepped out onto the sidewalk. Mama's voice, sounding strangely altered, floated out of the gatepost. "Go well, my dear ones. See you on Thursday."

"Say good-bye to Mama—here—in front of this square thing," Papa told her.

Rebecca stood on tiptoe and called into the metal grille on the gatepost, "Good-bye, Mama."

"Good-bye, little one," Mama's voice came back.

WITH Betty asleep on her lap, Rebecca drowsed, leaning against Papa as the *kombi* sped them back home. The tall buildings of the town were left behind. There was so much to tell Granny and John about her day. . . . Of the white people she had met, she liked only the magician. His face was kind, but though he smiled a lot his expression stayed sad. She wondered what made a magician sad. She wondered how the frog had got into her pocket without her knowing. She liked the baby too. . . . He reminded her of Noni's baby brother. Babies were all the same . . . they didn't seem to be different colors, black or white, like bigger children. Babies were just babies. . . . And the magic gate, John would be surprised to hear about that. She wouldn't tell them, though, about the way that white girl spoke to Mama. . . .

Papa nudged her into wakefulness. "The sea, Rebecca—"

She straightened up and looked out of the window. The evening sky was a clear, watery green, with streaks of purple cloud drifting across like smoke. Where the sky and sea met, the dark water shimmered with pink and orange light from the glow of the sunset. The fishing boats, the seagulls, had all gone home before darkness fell.

As the *kombi* traveled inland, the setting sun turned the sky crimson and gold as if a great fire burned somewhere beyond the darkening *veld*.

10

THE NEXT THURSDAY, Rebecca came home from school and found Mama already there. She'd been able to get off early, as her madam was going to be out all day at a tennis party and Mama didn't have to wait to serve her lunch.

"It made my heart sore when I saw the house next door," Mama said. "No children playing in the yard. So empty and sad. As if someone has died."

"The little one is still upset," Granny told her.

"Are you playing with the other girls, Rebecca?" Mama asked.

"I do, sometimes. But it's not the same without Noni."

Mama shook her head, saying nothing.

All the same, with Mama home everything seemed less worrying and disturbing to Rebecca. Everyone was more cheerful. Mama had brought stewing meat for supper and a delicious smell rose from the pot where it steamed and bubbled.

Rebecca was hungry when they sat down for the evening meal. The others were talking, but she was enjoying the meat gravy and *putu* and not listening. She scraped her plate clean and waited for John to finish what he was saying so that she could ask for another helping. But his words caught her attention.

"Big Albert says they're not going to be able to move us," John told them. "He says the lawyers who are working on our case are telling governments in other countries—England, America, I forget where else—how they are trying to remove us from our homes. He says people are going to come here, to our village—newspaper people, television people—and they'll see what's happening, and they'll tell our story to the whole world." He looked at them around the table, a scoop of *putu* uneaten in his hand. "And *everyone* will hear it."

"If they hear our story, will that stop the bulldozers from coming?" Rebecca asked.

"Perhaps the government will be ashamed to do it, once they know they are being watched by people all over the world," Papa suggested.

"Too ashamed to chase us out then?"

"It's nothing to do with being ashamed," John said. "Big Albert says they're afraid that other countries will stop doing business here. The white people will lose a lot of money—and they don't want *that* to happen."

"So they'll let us stay then?" Rebecca persisted.

"I hope so," Mama said.

But the worry remained. Even when she forgot it for a while, it waited for her, like the *tsotsis*—the bad boys who played truant and smoked and drank beer and jumped out from hiding places to frighten children sometimes on the way back from school.

After supper she sat down to finish her homework. She was good at arithmetic, but she'd got a lot of sums wrong on a test and had to do them all over again. And yesterday Miss Molefe had given her a poor mark on her geography homework. She liked to be at the top of the class, but since Noni had gone, her schoolwork didn't seem to be so interesting or important. She knew her teacher wasn't pleased with her. *I hope all the sums are right this time*, she thought as she closed her books and went to bed. With Mama home, she fell quickly asleep.

THERE WAS a sound of knocking. *Bang, bang, bang* . . . Rebecca thought she must be dreaming. She opened her eyes and sat up. Everyone was asleep, the small bedroom hushed with the sound of even breathing. In the other room the clock ticked comfortingly.

Then it started up again—*knocking*. She wasn't dreaming; someone was banging on the door. Her heart seemed to tilt. She tightened her arms around her knees, stiff as a piece of wood. *They've come— they're here to chase us out and start bulldozing. . . .* She heard Granny muttering in the other room and the creak of the couch springs as she got up and went to the door. "Who is it?" A woman's voice answered and the bolt rattled open.

Rebecca let go of her knees and breathed out her held breath. *Not the bulldozers . . .* In the kitchen the woman was telling Granny something in a high, excited voice. Papa woke, groaned, listened for a moment, roused Mama, and the two of them got out of bed and went into the kitchen. John slept on.

Rebecca waited, listening. A candle was lit in the other room, and its wavering light sent huge shadows leaping into corners of the bedroom. The woman's voice sounded familiar. Rebecca crept out of bed and went to stand in the doorway. Mama and Papa and Granny were standing around someone seated at the table. She lifted her face, tearstained in the flicker of the candlelight, and Rebecca saw who it was. *Miriam.* Noni's auntie Miriam who used to live next door with her family.

How had she got here from Pofadderkloof in the middle of the night? Rebecca wondered. She crossed the kitchen and went to stand beside Mama, clenching a fold of her mother's nightgown in her fist.

"Rebecca—my child!" Auntie Miriam shrieked. "Oh—my child—" She pulled her close and hugged her, her tears wetting Rebecca's face. "Oh—" she sobbed, "even the little ones—they even make the little ones suffer. Oh—Rebecca—how Noni misses you. She pines for you. Oh Lord . . ." she wailed, shoulders heaving with her distress.

"Shh . . . shh . . ." Mama calmed her. Granny made tea. They all sat around the table and listened to Auntie Miriam's story.

LATER, when everyone had gone back to bed, Auntie Miriam, exhausted, sharing the couch with Granny, Rebecca lay awake thinking about what she had heard. Beside her, Betty lay tucked up under the blankets.

Mama had been right. Noni's family had been warned that they were not allowed to tell anyone at all that they'd agreed to be moved. Even the children were cautioned not to say a word. "It sounded so good," Auntie Miriam had explained, once she had stopped crying and had some tea and bread. "My sister loved the idea of a bigger house, where the children would not have to be sleeping on the floor. We were so crowded next door—we didn't have room to turn around. And she was so tired from having to fetch water all day long from the public tap—all day long carrying those heavy buckets. Honestly, you can't blame her. She convinced my brother-in-law and me that it would be best for us if we went. They promised us there would be jobs. They said a fruit-canning factory was opening near Pofadderkloof and they would be needing lots of workers. Oh . . ." she wailed, tears starting up again and rolling down her round, pretty cheeks, "oh, how we hated to creep off like that—stealing away in the night like thieves, without saying good-bye to our beloved friends. But what could we do?"

Sniffing, wiping away the tears that kept coming, she told them of their truck ride through the night with all their household possessions piled around them and the little ones crying. At dawn, they came to Pofadderkloof.

"And you found it was all lies?" Granny asked.

"All lies." Solemnly, Auntie Miriam nodded.

"I knew it," Granny said. "I knew it all along."

There were houses there, Miriam told them. Brick houses, all new. They were allocated a house with two bedrooms and a kitchen. And a cold water tap.

"Electricity?" Papa asked.

"No electricity," she told them. "Nothing. No lights. No stove. Just a sink with a cold tap in the kitchen." They were told that in time there would be electricity, but the power lines hadn't been laid yet. The people from the planning department had unloaded their household goods from the truck and dumped them in front of the house; they were given a free sack of *mealie meal*, and the truck drove off.

As the sun rose, they looked about them and saw row upon row of houses and nothing but the bare, flat *veld* all around them. Later they found that only about twenty of the houses were occupied. The neighbors were all sad, hungry, without work, with nowhere to go.

"It was all lies," Granny said again.

"All lies," Auntie Miriam echoed. Building the canning factory hadn't been started. People couldn't go and look for work elsewhere, as there were no buses, no *kombis*.

"Does Noni go to school?" Rebecca asked.

There was a school building, Auntie Miriam told them. But there were no desks, no blackboards, no books or pencils or paper. "The children just sit on the floor and look at the teacher. And what can the teacher do?" She threw up her hands.

The neighbors told them that when they complained to the planning department, they were told they should be patient; there would be school equipment, jobs, a clinic, a church, all in good time. What shall we do until then? they had asked. Be patient, they were told.

"All lies," Granny intoned in the way she chanted *Amen* in church.

"All lies." Auntie Miriam shook her head. "Patience!" she declared with anger. "You know me. I have no patience to sit still and wait. And I have no patience with lies! I couldn't stand being with all those miserable people day after day, everyone lonely and sad and homesick. Even my sister's wild little boys are quiet now. Not fighting. Not playing. Just sitting there with big, hungry eyes."

"Did you see all the snakes there?" Rebecca asked.

"Snakes?"

"*Pofadders.*"

"Pofadderkloof!" Auntie Miriam said with scorn. "Even snakes wouldn't remain in such a bare, miserable place. And neither would I!"

She'd made up her mind to leave before the week was up. Her sister begged her to stay; but she couldn't remain there, she said, idle, becoming more miserable every day. She told Noni she was going, but not the boys. Her heart was sore but she had to go, she said. After the boys were in bed one night she packed a few things into a small bag and left, the sound of her sister's weeping still in her ears. She headed for the main road, which was a good distance from Pofadderkloof. It was very late, and she was thinking she might have to lie down and sleep in the *veld* at the side of the road, when, luckily, a black man came along in a small farm cart pulled by a donkey. He took her with him and she spent the night with the man's family in their hut on the farm where he worked. Next morning she had set out again, walking, hitching rides mostly from black truck drivers, and at last reached the town. She had given most of her money to her sister; after buying something to eat, she didn't have bus fare, so she had walked all the way from the town to the village. Her feet were hurting and she was worn out. All her bones ached, she said, and at the sight of the house next door where they had all lived together for so many years, empty now and abandoned, she had burst into tears. But even while she grieved for her sister's family so desolate at Pofadderkloof, she was thankful to be in the village again. She said that tomorrow she was going to the old people's home to ask if she could have her old job back.

"Tomorrow, first thing," Papa told her, "before you go anywhere, go straight to Big Albert and tell him everything you've told us. Perhaps he'll go to Pofadderkloof. It is important for him to know the truth. There's a big protest meeting at the end of the month, and if Albert can see for himself how it is there, he'll be able to confront the planning committee with their own lies."

JOHN never once stirred. "That boy sleeps like a stone," Mama had remarked as she climbed into the old iron bed with its creaky springs. Everyone slept now; it was very late, but still Rebecca lay awake. She couldn't stop thinking about Noni in that miserable place, her little brothers too sad to be naughty any more.

Noni had sent her a present. Auntie Miriam had been unpacking her small bag when she said, "Oh, I nearly forgot. Rebecca, Noni has sent something for you. She says it's for your doll." It was a little necklace made of tiny colored beads. "An old lady at Pofadderkloof is teaching Noni to make beaded straw tablemats. On weekends the old lady goes and sits beside the main road trying to sell her mats to people driving by. When I told Noni I was coming back here, she took some of the beads and made this for your dolly."

Betty was wearing the necklace as she lay asleep next to Rebecca. Even though Auntie Miriam hadn't seen any snakes, they still slipped through Rebecca's mind when she thought of Pofadderkloof. *Which is worse?* she wondered, *to be safe from the bulldozers in that miserable place—or to wait here, wondering all the time if they are coming to flatten the village.*

11

ON THE LAST Sunday of the month Mama arrived home earlier than usual. "There are posters about the meeting all over the village," she said.

"That's John's good work," Papa told her.

"We were up late last night making banners and placards, Mama," John said. "And I'm not even tired."

"He's too excited to be tired," Granny observed.

"Can I carry a placard?" Rebecca asked.

"No, little one. You must stay home with Granny," Papa answered.

"Why can't I come with you?"

"There will be a lot of people," Mama said. "I don't want you to be crushed in the crowd."

"What if you're crushed?"

"I won't be. I'm a big, strong woman."

Auntie Miriam was staying with them now. She slept on the kitchen floor on a foam-rubber pad that was rolled up each morning and pushed out of sight under the couch. She had got her job back at the old people's home. "You should see how glad those old white men and women are that I'm back," she told Rebecca. " '*Miriam, Miriam,*' they say, '*we missed you so much. Don't go away again.*' " Every week, when she got her wages, she would pay Granny her share of the household expenses as soon as she got home.

The demonstration was set for three in the afternoon. In the morning Rebecca went to church with Mama and Granny and Auntie Miriam.

Papa and John went to Big Albert's house. Papa was to be sitting on the speakers' platform. Albert had asked him to say a few words. Papa had said, "I'll do my best."

AFTER the service was over, Mr. Lekota the preacher told the congregation that they should all make sure the demonstration was a peaceful one. "We must all remain calm," he said. "We must give the police no excuse to use violence. Our cause is just. We are asking only to be left in peace in the place where we belong and which belongs to us."

When they came out of the small brick church building there were police cars driving slowly through the streets of the village, and many people, white and black, bustling around with cameras and notebooks.

"Who are they?" Rebecca asked Mama.

"They are from the newspapers and television. They are reporters."

"Just imagine, Rebecca," Auntie Miriam said excitedly. "People from all over the world will be able to see us on their televisions. They'll see how this government is trying to push us out of our homes." She adjusted the collar of her dress, jangled her earrings, and smiled into the cameras.

"Auw!" Granny grumbled at her. "What are you doing, Miriam? Do you think you are a film star?"

Soon Mr. Lekota was surrounded by reporters pushing and shouting questions at him, their cameras whirring, flashbulbs exploding. He had taken a baby from someone and held it in his arms, and he gathered a few children around him. Rebecca stood close to him and he patted her head while he spoke.

"I don't believe God approves of the way the government is trying to force us out of this village," he said calmly. "We will not be uprooted and dumped with our possessions in a barren place that is strange to us. I am building a new church for my congregation. Whatever they do, I am not moving. They must shoot me first because I am going nowhere. If they want to shoot me, they can shoot."

"I DON'T WANT them to shoot Mr. Lekota," Rebecca said as they walked home from church.

"They won't shoot him, child," Mama said. "He said that to show he's not afraid."

"Fancy so many television people coming here to our village," Auntie Miriam said. "And you were standing right next to Mr. Lekota, Rebecca. Do you realize that tomorrow people watching the news all over the world will see you? It's lucky you're wearing your nice blue dress."

"They'll see you too, Miriam," Granny said. "I saw how you were craning your neck so that you'd also be in the picture."

Mama laughed. "Why not? Why shouldn't people all over the world have a chance to see Miriam's pretty face?"

Rebecca had seen television once, long ago when she had visited Mama at her job. She had stood for a few minutes in the doorway of the room where the madam's husband was watching a game of soccer—tiny figures chasing a tiny ball over a field. He'd asked her if she wanted to come in to watch, but she had felt too shy and had gone back to Mama in the kitchen. Now she walked along between Mama and Auntie Miriam, worrying in case Mr. Lekota should be shot; that was more real to her than television.

REBECCA sat on the doorstep with Betty that afternoon, watching the crowds of people streaming by on their way to the large field near the church. Many carried placards and banners. She read some: "We Will Not Be Moved," "Save Our Village," "Keep the Bulldozers Out," "We Shall Overcome."

She wished she didn't have to stay home with Granny, but at the same time she didn't want to be pushed about in a great crowd where she was too small to see anything but the legs of grown-ups.

Granny watched with her for a while. When the crowds had all passed, she said, "I hope the police don't use tear gas."

"Tear gas? What is tear gas, Granny?"

"It's some stuff—like clouds—that they spray over crowds when they want to chase everyone away. It makes your eyes burn so that you think you're going blind, and it's like fire on your skin."

"Did it ever happen to you?" she asked, worrying about Mama and Papa and John and Auntie Miriam.

"No, child. But when I worked in town, some people I knew were at a meeting in one of the townships and the police used tear gas. They told me how it feels." Granny turned from the doorway and sat at the kitchen table to read her Bible.

The streets were quiet, empty. Except for some small children and old people, everyone seemed to be at the meeting. Rebecca sat with her arms clasping her knees, waiting. Waiting for her family to come home. Betty lay beside her on the step, but Rebecca didn't feel like playing with her or reading. She could only wait, very still, as if she really were with them at the meeting even while she sat on the step.

The sound of voices began to break like waves over the silent streets, echoing through crackling loudspeakers and followed by a great burst of cheers and roaring. Rebecca sat listening, looking up the road, wanting—from her toes to the top of her head— wanting to see Mama and Papa and John and Auntie Miriam come walking home. She kept watching the sky to see if tear gas would appear in a cloud of gray.

"Come inside, child," Granny called from the kitchen. "I'll make you a cup of tea."

"I'll have tea with them when they get back," she answered. She picked Betty up and fingered the little necklace of red and blue beads around her neck, waiting, waiting. The sky remained blue, cloudless. A small wind sprang up, shaking the fronds of the jacaranda tree and cooling Rebecca's face and arms, and on the wind came the sound of singing. Listening, she heard the strains of a song sung by many voices passing over the rooftops, its power and fullness moving through the feathery green of the jacaranda, spreading out over the *veld* and beyond the *koppies*. *Nkosi Sikalel' iAfrika*, God Save Africa, the hymn of the black people. Rebecca could sing it— she knew all the words. "They're singing *Nkosi Sikalel'*, Granny," she called out.

"That means the meeting's over." Granny came and stood in the doorway. "Thank God it's been peaceful. They'll be back soon now. I'll go and put the kettle on."

Rebecca went to wait at the gate, watching the road as the first trickle of people started to return to their houses, in twos and threes, then in larger groups, talking loudly, cheerfully. Impatient to see Mama and the others, she went and stood outside the gate, peering up the road. Where were they? . . . Why were they so slow getting back? . . . The crowds were beginning to thin. . . . At last she saw them. She ran along to meet them—Mama and John and Auntie Miriam. As she took Mama's hand she felt the grip of the afternoon fall away from her. "You're the last ones to come back. I've been waiting such a long time! Granny's just making tea." She trotted along beside them, holding onto Mama. "When's Papa coming?"

No one answered her. She looked up at Mama. As soon as she saw her face she knew something was wrong. "Where's Papa?" she asked.

Mama strode along, saying nothing.

"Where's Papa?"

"They arrested him," John said in a tight voice.

Rebecca burst into tears.

GRANNY made tea. No one spoke, all of them sipping the hot, sweet, milky tea for comfort while the clock ticked loudly away. A bee tumbled in and out of the geraniums on the windowsill as if nothing was wrong. Fear was inside the house now, Rebecca knew; the black snakes had got in. But the bee cared only about the sweetness in the flowers. Granny stirred the spoon in her tin mug, round and round, staring down past the table at something only she could see.

"*Why didn't they arrest me!*" John exploded, breaking the silence. "Papa was at work every day. *I* was the one working for Albert's committee—making posters, pasting them up everywhere. All kinds of things I did—why did they have to arrest *him*?"

"*He* made a speech," Auntie Miriam said.

"Only a short one."

"But everyone cheered him for a long time," Auntie Miriam said.

"And I was sitting here thanking God there'd been no trouble," Granny murmured.

"There *was* no trouble," Auntie Miriam told her. "It was a peaceful meeting. There were so many television cameras and newspaper people that the police wouldn't have dared lift a finger. They weren't going to start beating people up and using their guns and tear gas for all the world to see them on television."

"There were *hundreds* of police," John added. "Police, police, wherever you looked."

Mama sat silent, as if she were not even among them.

"So what happened?" Granny asked. "Why did they take your father?"

"They waited until the meeting was over and the television people had packed up their cameras and the reporters were all leaving. Then they surrounded the platform where all the speakers were, still talking to one another. . . . Most people didn't even see what was happening. They arrested every one of them. All eight."

"Even Big Albert?" Rebecca asked.

"He was the first one they took. I saw it all," John said. "I was standing next to the platform helping Eddie Nkwana take down the loudspeakers. Papa saw me. He waved to me when they were pushing him into the police van."

Granny made a choking sound and hastily took a gulp of tea.

Papa and Big Albert—both arrested . . . Big Albert knew how to speak to lawyers, to officials. He wasn't afraid of white people. Probably even Mama's madam would have to listen when he spoke. And he knew what had to be done. He knew how to arrange it so people on the other side of the world could watch and see what was happening in their small village. The television was like a magic eye that could protect them. But now—with Big Albert and Papa in jail—who would take care of them? . . . The government could come in the dark with its bulldozers. . . . Bad things could happen, and no one would know about them.

She went and sat on Mama's lap, but even as Mama held her in her firm, strong arms, Rebecca could feel how she sat stiffly, tensed with her worry about Papa, more like a chair than a person.

There was a knock at the door. A white man's voice called out, "May we come in?" Rebecca slipped quickly off Mama's lap. Three people—a black woman, an Indian man, and a white man—walked into the house.

"Mrs. Gwala?" the black woman inquired.

Mama nodded.

"We're the lawyers for the Committee to Save the Village," the woman said.

"They arrested my husband," Mama said.

"That's why we're here," the white man said.

"Make room, children." Granny stood up. "John—get the other chair from the bedroom. Come and sit down," she told the visitors. "Would you like some tea?"

They sat at the table. Granny served tea. Rebecca couldn't stop staring at the woman. She had thought that all lawyers must be white men. This lawyer was so pretty. She wore a dark suit with a white blouse and great gold hoop earrings.

"What am I to do?" Mama asked.

The woman put her hand on Mama's. "We think he'll be all right, Mrs. Gwala. There has been so much publicity about this removal—international publicity—that it's unlikely any of them will come to harm. And being arrested with Big Albert Kosane will also protect them, because Albert is so well known."

"Albert was on television yesterday," the white

lawyer told them. "The program wasn't allowed to be seen here in our country, of course. But he was on news services all over the world. He was taking reporters around Pofadderkloof—showing that what the government has promised there is all lies."

"I was the one—" Auntie Miriam broke in with her wide smile, dimples showing—"I was the one who told Big Albert how it is all lies."

Rebecca wondered if Noni had been in the television pictures of Pofadderkloof.

"You were there?" the Indian lawyer asked. "At Pofadderkloof?"

Auntie Miriam nodded so vigorously that her earrings danced and tinkled. "And I ran away when I saw what it was like," she said with pride.

"They haven't come looking for you?" he asked. Rebecca watched how the point of his beard waggled as he spoke.

Auntie Miriam shook her head. "They can come with a whole herd of elephants, but they won't be able to drag me back to that place," she told him.

The white lawyer spoke. "We've come to tell you that we'll be working on the case. We'll try to have them out of jail as soon as possible." He was round and jolly looking, and he kept running his hands through his rumpled gray hair; though he was fat and much older, he reminded Rebecca in some way of the magician—how he had told her to look in her pocket and the magic frog would be there. "Of course," he went on, "we don't know how long it will take, weeks—months perhaps—but we'll be doing everything that can be done."

"It was a peaceful gathering." The Indian lawyer pounded his fist on the table so that the teaspoons rattled in the tin mugs. "People asserting their right not to be thrown out of their homes," he said with a scowl, "and they are arrested. It's a scandal."

"They're trying to scare the rest of us," John said.

"That's what we believe," the lady lawyer said.

John's fingers were clenched. Rebecca could see that he was near to tears. "What kind of people are these—arresting somebody just because he won't stand by and allow his house to be knocked down by a bulldozer!" he cried out.

"*Hau*," Granny sighed. "Trouble—trouble—so much trouble. . . . Why don't they just let us live in peace?"

"We'll live in peace one day, Granny," the lady lawyer said. "One day we'll have a decent life. But it's a struggle; they won't give it to us."

Her words gave Rebecca a feeling of comfort. She trusted what this lady was telling them; she was clever, she was black like they were, and she cared about what was happening in their village. Rebecca wondered if she could be a lawyer when she grew up. She would wear a smart suit and blouse just like that, and earrings, and carry a leather briefcase.

With the three lawyers in the house Rebecca felt

protected again. They explained what they'd have to do to get Papa and the others out of jail. Their words went to and fro across the table but Rebecca couldn't follow them. She noticed that John wasn't upset any more. He was listening as if his ears wanted to catch every word being said.

Tiring of the talk, she went into the bedroom to play with Betty. She dressed her in a yellow dress, and for a sash she tied a red satin ribbon she had brought home from the birthday party.

"COME HERE, my child, and say good-bye," Mama called. The white lawyer smiled at Rebecca, cupping her chin in his hand. She could see the buttons on his shirt straining to burst open against the bulge of his stomach. "We'll try and get your daddy back to you soon, sweetheart," he said.

"Say thank you, Rebecca," Mama told her.

"Thank you," she said. She liked this white man—he was kind. Mama's madam seemed kind, but all the time she cared only about herself. This man came to their village and sat in their kitchen and wanted to help them.

The Indian lawyer said, "There'll be a problem with money while your husband is in jail, Mrs. Gwala. There is a fund to assist the families of arrested people." He wrote on a square of paper. "This is the address of the office in town. Go and see them, and they will help you."

"Where do they get the money from?" Auntie Miriam asked.

"People send money," the lady lawyer said. "People from all over the world." Gently, she brushed her hand over Rebecca's head. "Try not to be frightened, little one," she said. "We have friends everywhere."

"Mrs. Gwala," the white lawyer said, standing to leave, "your husband's speech was simply wonderful." He took her hands in both of his. "You can be proud of him. Everyone was moved. I saw one television cameraman wiping tears from his eyes."

"It's because his heart was speaking for him," Auntie Miriam said.

Mama shook her head in wonder. "You know— he's never spoken in public before."

"And now," Auntie Miriam said, "they'll see him and hear him in England, in America, in France, everywhere."

Standing among them by the door, Rebecca wondered how television worked. It must be some kind of magic, she thought, like the magician did at the party. Television could show their troubles to people all over the world, could show her father making a speech.

"What did Papa say at the meeting?" she asked Mama later.

John answered. "He talked about you," he said.

"About me!"

John nodded. "He told how he'd taken you to visit Mama in town. How Mama's madam has a girl the same age as you, who lives without fear because no one is telling her family that they have to move, no one is threatening to bulldoze their house. Yet every night you're afraid, he said, because tomorrow the bulldozers might come. He said a father has no choice but to protect his children—even against the government, if it is planning to harm them."

Rebecca's eyes filled with tears.

"*Hau*," Granny said. "I would have liked to hear him." She set about preparing supper.

But no one felt like eating.

106

12

MAMA DIDN'T GO back to work in the dark next morning. The lawyers had told her that first thing she should go to the supermarket where Papa worked and explain to his boss what had happened; she should tell them that lawyers were working on his case, and ask them to hold his job for him until he came out of jail.

"I'll phone my madam as soon as I get into town and tell her what has happened," Mama said as they had their bread and tea. "The master will be so mad when he comes downstairs and finds his breakfast isn't on the table."

"Can't the baby's nanny make the breakfast?" Rebecca asked.

"She can, I suppose. But Madam doesn't like her to do the cooking."

"Let them get their own breakfast for a change!" John snapped. "What's the matter with those people? They're not cripples, are they?"

"They can't do anything for themselves," Mama answered. "They're not used to it."

"Then they'd better get used to it," John said. "Someday, soon, they're not going to have us taking care of them as if they're babies."

"What will we be doing instead, John?" Rebecca wanted to know.

"We'll be taking care of ourselves. This will be *our* country—not theirs."

"Where will they go?" Rebecca asked in surprise.

"Oh," John said, looking important, "they can stay if they like—but *we* won't be doing their work for them any more. They can clean up their own mess and cook for themselves, and Mama will stay home and look after her own family."

"Oh, John . . ." Rebecca said, filled with longing. "When will that be?"

"I don't know—quite soon, I think."

"Off you go, children," Granny said. "No time for dreaming. You'll be late for school."

As soon as all the children were seated in their desks, Miss Molefe said, "Listen now, everyone. I want you all to know that Rebecca's father was arrested yesterday, along with Big Albert Kosane and six others. Her father made a very fine speech at the meeting. He is a brave man trying to help us all. Let's give Rebecca a big hand now."

Miss Molefe clapped her hands and all the children

in the class joined in. They stared at Rebecca and smiled at her; she felt very shy, but proud at the same time.

When the clapping was over, Rebecca said in a small voice, "The lawyers came to our house last night. They are working on his case, to get him out of jail."

"What did she say?" some children called out. "Speak louder, Rebecca—we can't hear you."

But Rebecca was too embarrassed to repeat it, so Miss Molefe told them what she had said, adding that they all hoped her father would be home very soon. Then they got on with their lessons.

AUNTIE MIRIAM had a phone call from Mama at the old people's home. When she got back in the evening she told the family that Mama wouldn't be coming next Thursday, as she had to go to the office in town where they helped the families of arrested people; she would need to get money from them so they'd be able to buy food while Papa was in jail. She told Miriam she'd been to see Papa's boss at the supermarket. He said that since Papa had been with them for so long, they'd hold his job, but they would have to hire someone else until he was released from prison. They would stop his pay until he returned to work.

"And how long will that be?" Granny said, with a shake of her head.

"The greediness of those people makes me so mad!" John exclaimed. "That supermarket makes a lot of their money from black people who shop there—yet they can't pay a man when he's put in jail for trying to protect his own family from the bulldozers." He clasped his hand over his clenched fist and hammered at the air. "It makes me want to *smash* something."

"Calm down, Johnny," Auntie Miriam told him. "Those people aren't so bad. They gave your mother a present of twenty *rand*."

"Twenty *rand*!" John said scornfully. "That's how much the boss's wife pays for a bottle of *perfume*. In town once I saw in the window of a chemist's shop —there was a tiny bottle of perfume for twenty *rand*. It's *nothing* to them."

"Oh, Johnny," Auntie Miriam laughed. "You're such a funny boy. You're like a firecracker—we never know when you're going to go *bang*."

"I'm not joking, Auntie Miriam," he answered. "I mean what I say."

SOMETIMES, after school, a group of girls would stop by the house to ask Rebecca to come and play. When she stumbled in a skipping-rope game, they gave her a second chance; and at hopscotch, when she threw her stone and it fell on the line marked in the dust, they said it was still inside the square and she could go on playing. She shared some of the ribbons and rosettes from the party with them. But in spite of their friendliness, she wished and wished that Noni was still living next door; with Papa in jail she felt lonelier than ever without her.

And there was mostly *putu* without meat or gravy to eat now. The small sum of money Mama got from the office in town didn't go very far; everything cost so much, she said. The neighbors were kind and brought gifts of food—packets of tea, *mealies*, fruit, bread, whenever they had a little to spare. But because seven others besides Papa had been jailed, whatever food there was had to be shared among many.

WHEN Mama came home on her next Sunday off she looked tired and worried. She told them that the lady lawyer had phoned her at work to say she could visit Papa at the jail the following Thursday afternoon. The call had made her anxious, as she thought it meant they were going to be keeping him imprisoned for a long time. The lawyer had told her there was to be a court hearing, and they had applied for the charges to be dismissed. She told her that there was a lot of protest from governments around the world about the arrests and the threatened removal to Pofadderkloof. Mama sighed. "But she told me it's hard to tell how long it will take before they're released."

"Are they showing about Papa on the television?" Rebecca asked.

"Not here," John said. "We're not supposed to know anything. But overseas—we've heard there's often something on television about the case."

111

"Johnny, you're getting so clever," Auntie Miriam said, looking at him with admiration. "How do you know all this?"

"Those who were working with Big Albert's committee have formed a new one now that he's in jail," he explained. "The police think that if they lock up the leaders then the protest will quiet down and they'll be able to move us all to Pofadderkloof. But there are new leaders to take their place. And they keep in touch with others who know what's happening in the world outside our village. And the more the world outside knows what's going on, the safer we are. This government has a very bad name overseas, Auntie Miriam. They don't want it to be known what cruel things they do to us."

Granny, stirring her pot, looked over her shoulder at John. "You're not a boy any more, Johnny. These troubles are turning you suddenly into a man."

He didn't say anything, but Rebecca could see that he was pleased.

"You even look taller than when I was last home," Mama said. "Papa will be proud of you, Johnny, when I tell him what you're doing." She sighed deeply. "But don't get into any trouble, my boy—it's too much for me."

"Don't worry, Mama. When you see Papa just tell him we're not going to lie down for the bulldozers to roll over us. And tell him, since the protest meeting, not one more family has moved to Pofadderkloof."

"Trouble . . . trouble . . ." Granny murmured, as if she were talking to the old blackened pot.

❧ REBECCA missed Mama the minute she was gone. And it would be two weeks before she saw her again. In the mornings before school, her stomach hurt, but it was no use telling Granny—she wouldn't allow her to stay home. In class, she lost her place in the book when Miss Molefe called on her to read out loud, and she started getting her sums wrong. Miss Molefe was kind to her and didn't scold, but every day Rebecca had to bring her arithmetic book home and do the sums over again.

In the afternoons, she stayed under the jacaranda tree with Betty and read the bear stories. The summer was passing. The blue flowers had gone from the tree. She remembered how she and Noni had always had fun with the flowers, slipping them over the tips of their fingers, threading them into necklaces. They would wiggle their toes in the fallen blossoms, cool and soft under their bare feet, as if they were stepping into a real pool. Rebecca always sat, now, with her back turned to Noni's empty house.

One afternoon, Betty lay asleep in her box; Rebecca didn't lift her out or change her clothes. Instead, she leaned against the trunk of the tree, a book open on her lap, thinking about the time she had let Betty stay overnight at Noni's house. Then she turned the pages of the book, looking at the pictures of the bear's birthday party, and remembered the sad face of the magician at the white children's party.

The gate opened. It squeaked loudly now that Papa wasn't home to oil it as he regularly did. John was home—and in a bad mood, Rebecca saw. He kicked at a pebble, and it landed in Betty's box.

"Look what you're doing, John," Rebecca complained.

"Why do you play with that stupid white doll?" John retorted. "Those whites are the cause of all our trouble. *They* put Papa in jail. *They* want to chase us out of our homes. How can you play with one of *their* dolls, Rebecca! You haven't got any sense."

Rebecca snatched Betty out of the box and clutched her to her chest. "Leave me alone! I *have* got sense." She felt tears of anger rising, filling her eyes. "She's *my* doll. I don't care *what* color she is. There's nothing wrong with her. *She* hasn't done anything wrong."

"I'd like to pull her arms and legs off."

"*No! No!*" Rebecca screamed, scrambling to her feet and backing away from her brother.

Granny appeared in the doorway. "*John*, stop teasing your sister."

"I'm not teasing her. I'm trying to teach her something."

"Never mind that," Granny said. "Leave her alone and go and fill the bucket for me like a good boy."

John went inside to fetch the bucket; he came out again and went to the public tap without saying anything more.

Rebecca sat Betty on her lap so that her blue eyes opened. She seemed to be staring at Rebecca as if to say, "I haven't done anything wrong." Rebecca changed her into her nightdress, cradling her in her arms so that her eyes closed, and softly sang a lullaby that Granny used to sing to her when she was little.

Granny called her in to do her homework. Rebecca hadn't been paying attention in class while Miss Molefe showed them how to do some new sums. Now, each time she checked one she came up with a different answer, and she used the eraser so often that the pages became grubby and creased. She was still working at her arithmetic by the time Auntie Miriam came in from work.

"Oh child, why do you look so worried?" Miriam exclaimed. She hugged her close. "Is your homework so hard for you tonight?"

"John has been teasing her," Granny said.

"I wasn't teasing," John protested. "I just told her it's not right for a black child to play with a white doll, that's all."

"Oh Johnny." Auntie Miriam sat down and kicked off her high-heeled red shoes. "Everything is hard enough with your father in jail. Leave the child alone and let her play with her doll in peace."

"None of you understands politics," John said crossly.

"The best politics is the kind that lets people live in peace," Granny said from the stove.

13

TWO LONG WEEKS before Mama would be home again. Rebecca went about feeling tired all day. But the nights were worse, and the bad dreams crowded in again, though when she woke in the mornings they had fled before she could remember them. Granny looked at her and shook her head and said she didn't like the dark shadows under her eyes; she sighed, and stroked Rebecca's head.

"She's pining for her mama and papa," Auntie Miriam said.

Granny sighed again, and said nothing.

"I think the child ought to be drinking fresh milk," Auntie Miriam decided, and every evening now she came home with a carton of milk for Rebecca.

Rebecca drank the milk, but it didn't make her feel any better.

ON THE Sunday Mama was due to come home. Rebecca was up so early that even Granny was still asleep behind the drawn curtains of her cubicle. In the cool of the fresh morning she waited, swinging to and fro on the squeaky gate, her feet slipped into two spaces where the wire chain links had worked loose over the years she and Johnny had swung there. Granny called her to come in for breakfast, but she said she would wait until Mama came.

When at last she saw her mother's familiar form, weighed down with plastic shopping bags, coming slowly down the road, she flew out to meet her, running so fast that she could have won a race. Mama bent down to hug her and all the shopping bags swung around Rebecca's shoulders, creaking and rustling.

"Are you all right, little one?" Mama asked as they walked to the house. "I've missed you so much that my heart feels sore."

"Oh, Mama—I'm so glad you're here. Did you see Papa? How does he look? When will he be coming home? Is it soon?" Rebecca clung to Mama's dress, not wanting to let go of her now that she was here.

Mama laughed. "Such a lot of questions. Let me get into the house at least and put these heavy bundles down."

Mama's madam had sent food for the family. When the bags were unpacked the table was full of good things to eat. Granny cooked eggs with bacon, and there was a loaf of fresh bread. They all gathered around to eat a late breakfast while Mama told about her visit to the jail.

"Papa looks all right. His cell is small and crowded, but Big Albert keeps their spirits up. He says the food is terrible."

"I wish I could give him my eggs and bacon," Rebecca said.

"Eat it up," Granny said. "You need it."

"But he's in good spirits," Mama went on. "He says he's lucky to be in the same cell as Big Albert, because he's learning a lot from him."

"What is he learning?" John asked eagerly.

"Let me see . . . what did he tell me? He's learning about how things got to be the way they are in this country—with the whites taking all the best things for themselves and leaving nothing for us."

"What else?" John wanted to know.

"He talked about Nelson Mandela. Twenty-six years he's been in jail, only because he was working to try and free our people."

"Maybe they'll keep Papa for twenty-six years too," Rebecca said, her eyes filling with tears.

"No, no, child." Mama wiped the tears away. "Mandela wants to save all the black people. Papa was only speaking for our village."

"It's all part of the same thing," John said. "Was Papa allowed to say whatever he wanted, Mama?"

"There was a black prison guard. But he was quite nice and he didn't interfere."

"Huh!" John said. "How can he be nice when he's doing the work of the white people who are keeping Papa in jail!"

"Johnny," Auntie Miriam reprimanded him. "That prison guard probably has a wife and a lot of hungry children to feed. You shouldn't be so hard on people."

"Why can't he find a job then where he doesn't have to keep his black brothers locked up?" John retorted.

"It's true what you say, Johnny," Mama said. "But you know, it's not easy to find work. People take what they can get."

But Rebecca only wanted to hear about Papa. "When is he coming home?" she asked.

"There is going to be something, quite soon they hope, in the court. A hearing, it's called. The lawyers will explain to the judge that Papa and the others were wrongfully arrested, so he should let them go free."

"Then will he let them go free?" Rebecca asked.

"I hope so," Mama said. "They think there is a good chance because their case is getting worldwide attention."

Worldwide attention . . . Rebecca liked the sound of those words. When Mama said them it made her feel as if she was being looked after—as if those words connected them, somehow, to something strong and good, something larger and stronger than the government which wanted to chase them from the village and flatten their houses and take over the valley and the gently rising *koppies* for themselves. The three lawyers as well, she thought—the pretty black lady, the tall, thin Indian, the kind, fat white man—they were also part of the same kindness that would help and protect the people of the village. Knowing about them, and the *worldwide attention*, made her feel less alone and afraid.

In the evening when she was putting Betty to bed, she sang to her in a quiet voice so that the others in the next room wouldn't hear her. It was the tune of the lullaby Granny always sang, but she made up new words for it:

> *Go to sleep, little one,*
> *Sleep well.*
> *I want to mention*
> *There is worldwide attention.*
> *I want to mention*
> *There is worldwide attention.*
> *Sleep, little one,*
> *Sleep well.*

Mama came to tuck her into bed. "What are you singing to your dolly, Rebecca?"

"Just a tune. Will you be going to visit Papa again next Thursday, Mama?"

"No. Visits are allowed only once a month. Please God by next month he'll be out."

"So will you come home next Thursday?"

"If nothing else comes up, my girlie. Good night. Sleep well."

"Good night, Mama."

Rebecca lay down and just as soon as her eyes closed she was in a deep, quiet sleep.

EVERY MORNING at breakfast Rebecca asked, "Do you think the court hearing will be today?"

"Eat your breakfast and go to school," Granny told her. "What I think doesn't matter. If it did—your father wouldn't be in jail."

But the next morning, "Do you think the court hearing will be today?" she asked as soon as she sat down to her bread and tea.

"Every day I read the newspaper," Auntie Miriam said. "So far there has been nothing about it."

"Our committee will know before it's in the newspapers," John told them, looking important as he always did when he spoke about the committee. "Don't worry, Rebecca, I'll let you know in good time."

"I'm getting tired of waiting, John. And Mama. She hardly ever comes home on Thursdays now."

"She can't help it, Rebecca," John said. "She has to visit Papa, or see the lawyers, or go to the fund office to get money. D'you want to go hungry?"

"I don't care. I just want Mama and Papa here."

"The Sunday after this one, Mama will come."

Rebecca lived for the days her mother was home. Still there was no word of the hearing. Feeling sad became part of what she did every day. She got used to it. She didn't look forward to things anymore in the way that had made her happy and excited before Papa was arrested, before Noni went away. Now there was only one thing to wait for, and that was Papa getting out of jail. It was taking so long. Sometimes it was hard for Rebecca to imagine him home again. Even the fear of Pofadderkloof and the bulldozers had moved off where her worry could no longer reach it.

One morning in class, as Rebecca stared out of the window at John sitting with his group under the trees, Miss Molefe pulled a large map down over the blackboard for a geography lesson. "Now children, are you all listening? *Rebecca—pay attention.* Today I have something very important to show you. This is a map of the world. The *whole world.* All these are the continents—other lands. All this blue is the sea." With her wooden pointing stick she indicated an area that, to Rebecca, appeared to be shaped something like the head of an old elephant with a great, fat trunk. "This is Africa. And here—this whole lower part—is our country, South Africa. And right down here—" she pointed to a spot near the bottom of the elephant's trunk—"here, on the coast, this dot, is our own village. Here is where we are. Here is the sea. Here is the town. Here is our village. Do you all see it?"

"Yes, Miss Molefe," the children chorused.

"Now. Willie Tsomo, stop winding that toy up

or I'll take it away from you. Do you all see this area over here? This is America. This small island in the sea, here, is England. Here is Europe. Pay attention now. I have something important to tell you. Will you *stop* wriggling, Tommy Jabalala."

She waited for silence before she went on. "Now, children. You all know that Rebecca's father and Big Albert Kosane and six others are in jail, don't you?"

"Yes, Miss Molefe," the children called out, while Rebecca sat quiet, wondering what their teacher was going to tell them.

"And you all know why they are in jail?"

"Yes, Miss Molefe."

"Well, now, listen to me. There is soon going to be a court hearing. That means the lawyers will be telling the judge that these eight men should all go free because they have not done anything wrong. They have only tried to do right. And no one should be jailed for doing what is right. Do you follow me?"

"Yes, Miss Molefe."

"Well, children. All over the world there is a lot of interest in this case."

Rebecca put up her hand for permission to speak. "Worldwide attention," she said.

"Quite correct, Rebecca. The case is getting *worldwide attention*. And now we have heard something very encouraging. We've been told that five countries are each sending some very important people from their governments over here, to South Africa. They are going to sit in on the case and listen carefully to what is said and done. They will be here to make sure that eight innocent men are not going to be punished for protesting when our government tries to turn us out of our homes and take the land over for white people."

"*Amandla!*" a boy at the back of the class cheered, and all the children raised clenched fists and joined in the cheering, Rebecca as well.

Miss Molefe smiled. "All right. Quiet now. This is what I want to show you today in our geography lesson. These five people—observers, they're called —are coming from overseas, flying a long, long way to get here." She pointed at the map. "One from America, one from England, one from Holland, one from Germany, and one from Sweden—up here."

She turned to face them. "These five observers— even though we don't know them—know all about us. They know about our village, about Rebecca's father and the others in jail. So the judge is going to find it very difficult, *with them listening and watching*, to do anything that is *not right*. These five people all come from countries where there is only *one law* for *all* the people, no matter what color they are. . . . Now—"

She handed around sheets of paper that had the outline of the map of the world traced out on them and set them to filling in the names of all the continents and finding the countries from which the observers were coming.

During the morning break Rebecca went to find John in the school yard.

"John! Miss Molefe told us *observers* are coming from *overseas*."

"I know," he said. "It's good news! Joshua Kosane was at the school gate this morning, waiting to tell me." He was filled with excitement—as though he'd swallowed a whole dishful of it, Rebecca thought.

"But *when* is the hearing going to be?" she asked.

"Two weeks from today, Joshua says. That old judge is going to have to watch his step with those five sitting in his court, watching *him*."

"Tomorrow's Thursday. Mama's coming home. She'll be happy to hear about it, won't she, John?"

"*Everyone* will be happy," he answered.

The school bell rang. John squeezed Rebecca's hand and went to join his group under the trees. Rebecca ran across the school yard back to her class, humming to herself as she went: *I'd like to mention there is worldwide attention. . . .*

14

MAMA CAME HOME her next Sunday off and showed them a picture of the front page of a newspaper: some men stepping out of the side of an airplane. "Look. Here they are," she said, tapping the page.

Rebecca and Granny and John studied the grainy photo. "Who are they?" Rebecca asked.

"Three of the observers," Mama told them. "They've flown in from overseas for the court hearing."

Rebecca took the paper and looked closely at the picture, studying it for a long time. Three men in dark suits and ties. One of them was black, the other two white. She stared at them, wondering. What were their houses like? . . . Did they have children? Here they were, flown over the blue-colored sea from faraway lands to come and see that the right thing would be done, and then Papa could come home to them. . . . They would have to be good, she thought, to care about what happened to people they didn't even know. . . . Better than Mama's madam and master, and better than the men in the government who tried to chase people from their homes. Probably they were more like Big Albert and Mr. Lekota the preacher.

Mama had taken off her shoes and flopped down in Papa's armchair. "I'm so *tired*. I seem to be running all the time these days."

"Rest today," Granny told her. "I'll cook the food. You look worn out."

"Not much longer to wait," John said. "Next Wednesday's the hearing."

"That madam of mine!" Mama shook her head. "I told her: Madam—next week instead of Thursday I must be off on Wednesday, so that I can be at the court hearing. '*Oh, Martha*,' she says, 'you *know* I'm having a bridge party on Wednesday afternoon!' 'I'm sorry, Madam,' I told her, 'but I must be in court to hear how it goes.' So then she tries to tell me it will be a waste of time to go to court because nothing would happen. She says it will probably be *weeks* before the judge gives his decision on the case."

"Weeks!" Rebecca said. "I thought Papa would be coming home next Wednesday."

"That madam—what does she know!" John said with contempt. "Does she think she's a lawyer? All she knows is bridge and tennis. I hope you won't let her stop you from going, Mama."

"I told her that Papa will be glad just to see me sitting there in court. I told her I'm *going*. I said I'd do all the baking the day before, and the nanny and the gardener have promised they'll help out at the bridge party."

"So you'll be in court, Mama?" Rebecca asked.

"Certainly I will."

"I wonder how that *Mandy* would like it if her Papa was in jail," Rebecca remarked.

THE EVENING before the hearing, Granny was preparing supper while Rebecca sat over her homework. It was hard to keep her mind on her sums. *What will happen tomorrow in court?* she wondered.

"John won't be home for supper," Granny said. "He's helping make placards for the demonstration outside the court tomorrow." She looked at the clock. "I wonder what's happened to Miriam? She's late this evening. Perhaps the two of us should eat without her."

"I'd rather wait, Granny."

"Is your homework done? Why don't you work on your sewing then, until she comes."

Granny had shown Rebecca how to stitch a piece of blue satin ribbon around the hem of one of Betty's dresses. Rebecca fetched her sewing. "This can be her party dress," she said as she tried to sew without getting her thread in a tangle.

"Don't use such a long thread, child."

"The stitches just seem to want to come out big, Granny. Why can't I make them small and straight like yours?"

"Practice. They'll come smaller after a while."

The door flew open and Auntie Miriam bustled in. She was carrying a large silver shopping bag with pictures of colored balloons all over it. "Sorry! Sorry! Sorry I'm late. I had to pick up a parcel and I missed my usual *kombi* ride." Her eyes were shining, her cheeks dimpling.

"What a pretty shopping bag," Rebecca remarked. "What's in it, Auntie Miriam?"

"Oh," she replied, "something I've been paying off for a couple of months. Today was the day I'd arranged to pick it up."

"I hope you're not wasting your money on more clothes, Miriam," Granny scolded.

Auntie Miriam smiled. "It's not a dress, Granny."

"What is it?" Rebecca asked.

"Guess."

"How can I guess? . . . A new coat?"

"It's not for me." Auntie Miriam was smiling so that the tops of her round cheeks almost hid her eyes.

"Who is it for?" Rebecca asked.

"For you."

"For me!" Rebecca was astonished. She put down her sewing. "For me? What is it?"

Granny was setting the *putu* on the table. She paused, ladle in hand.

"Come and see," Auntie Miriam said.

Rebecca walked to the couch where Auntie Miriam was easing off her tight shoes. She stared at the package.

"Come on, child. Open it—it's yours."

Inside the shopping bag was an oblong box wrapped in shiny paper and tied with a red ribbon, just like the presents the white children had brought to Mandy's birthday party. "But Auntie Miriam . . . it's not my birthday."

"Better open it before the *putu* gets cold," Granny told her.

"Do *you* know what it is, Granny?"

"I know nothing about it," Granny said, while Auntie Miriam sat there, rubbing her cramped toes, enjoying the excitement she had brought into the house. She looked so pleased and plump and pretty that it seemed she might burst out of her close-fitting dress.

Kneeling, Rebecca lifted the box from the shopping bag. Very carefully, she untied the ribbon. Slowly she removed the paper, which was also silver with colored balloons all over. Granny took it from her and flattened and folded it into a neat square, watching with curiosity as Rebecca lifted the lid off a gray cardboard box. Inside, something was wrapped in layers of pink tissue paper.

She looked up at Auntie Miriam.

"Go on—unwrap it," Auntie Miriam urged.

Rebecca spread apart the rustling layers of tissue.

There, lying on its back, eyes closed, was a baby doll. A black baby doll.

"*Hau!*" Granny said softly.

Rebecca lifted it from the wrappings. Its eyes opened and it looked at her. They were dark brown eyes. Its head was covered with short black springing curls just like Rebecca's. The doll was dressed in a diaper and an undershirt and little knitted booties.

"Turn it over," Auntie Miriam said.

"*Mama,*" the baby doll cried.

Rebecca sat the doll upright on the couch and flung her arms around Auntie Miriam's neck, hugging her tightly. "Oh—Auntie Miriam—it's the best doll I ever saw—it's the best doll in the whole world. . . . Oh, Auntie Miriam—" She hugged her again.

Granny had picked the doll up and was inspecting it. "Aren't you going to say thank you?"

"Oh, Auntie Miriam—thank you, thank you, thank you."

Auntie Miriam laughed. "You're squeezing me to death, child."

"It looks just like Mrs. Chikane's new baby," Granny remarked.

"I wish Noni could see it," Rebecca said.

"What are you going to name her?" Auntie Miriam asked.

"Noni," Rebecca said at once.

She could hardly eat the supper Granny set before her, and kept playing with the doll on her lap.

"That time Johnny was teasing you because you

131

play with a white doll," Auntie Miriam explained while she ate, "I made up my mind to find you a black dolly. A friend of mine at work told me she had seen one in a toy shop near the station. The most trouble I had was keeping the secret to myself." She laughed. "And wasn't I just glad that today was the last payment and I could go and pick it up—the day before the court hearing. And now if they let him out, you'll be able to show your Papa—"

John appeared at the door. "Show Papa what?" he asked.

Rebecca ran to him with the new doll.

"That's better," he said, looking at it sternly. "Much better to play with a black doll. Now you can throw away that broken white doll those people threw *you* instead of throwing it in the rubbish bin where it belongs."

"No!" Rebecca cried. "I still like Betty. I won't throw her away."

John shook his head. "After everything the white people have done to us—putting your father in jail! Yet you'll still play with a white doll! Honestly, Rebecca—I don't know what's the matter with you."

"Sit down now, child. Eat your food and leave her alone," Granny said. "There's nothing the matter with her."

"Not all whites are the same, Johnny," Auntie Miriam told him. "What about that fat lawyer? And those people at that office who give your mother money for food—they're white. And four of those observers who've come from overseas are white."

"So why did you buy her a black doll then?" John demanded.

"Because I wanted her to have a black doll as well as a white one—that's all."

At bedtime Rebecca put the two dolls to sleep side by side in their box beds. "Good night Betty," she whispered so that John should not hear her. "Good night, Noni. Maybe tomorrow you'll be able to see Papa."

15

THE DAY of the court hearing came and went. In the newspaper, in a tiny corner at the bottom of the page, there was a report that the judge had heard the evidence and would announce at a later date whether Papa and the others were to stand trial or be set free.

When Mama came home on Sunday, she told them that there had been a small group of demonstrators outside the courthouse. "Papa waved and smiled at me from the prisoners' dock," she said. "I know he was really pleased I was there."

"And the observers?" John asked.

"They were listening and taking notes." Mama sighed. "They seemed like sensible people," she added.

She looked so weary, and Rebecca could tell she was heavy hearted though she tried to appear cheerful. They had hoped for a lot from the hearing, and nothing had changed. Even so, every day when Rebecca walked home from school she told herself she would find Papa sitting in his favorite chair. And every day she was disappointed.

Auntie Miriam read in the papers that the observers had all flown back to their own countries to report the case to their governments. In her mind Rebecca saw their planes flying to the different continents Miss Molefe had shown them on the map—one landing on a pink-colored country, another on a brown, on a green . . . with the seas all blue around them. But still Papa was in jail. The way it was now seemed the way it had always been.

IT SAID in the papers a while later that the government had now decided there were no longer going to be separate beaches for blacks and whites; black people would be allowed on all the beaches.

"We won't have to swim on that rocky beach any more?" Rebecca asked.

"What a big favor they think they're doing us!" John said angrily. "They keep Papa in jail. They keep *thousands* of people in jail. They try to push us out of the way so that whites can live here. They don't let black people vote. And they think we'll be happy now because we're allowed to swim on their beaches!"

"They're not *their* beaches," Granny said. "Beaches, the sea, the sky, don't belong to the government. They belong to God. They're for everyone."

Winter was coming on. The grass of the *veld* was yellowing, the trees standing bare among the falling leaves. The days were sunny but the nights were sharp and chilly and there wasn't enough money to buy kerosene for the heater. Indoors it was cold, and the harsh wind blew in through the cracks and spaces where the door and windows didn't fit properly. In the house they all wore extra sweaters and thick socks to try to keep warm, and Granny never took off the maroon knitted cap she wore pulled well over her ears, even when she went to bed at night.

On a Sunday, when she was buttoning Rebecca into her winter coat before they set out for church, Mama sighed and said, "This coat is too tight—and look how short the sleeves are."

"All the money Miriam wasted on that doll," Granny muttered. "It would have been better spent on a winter coat for the child."

"Oh no, Granny," Rebecca protested. "I'd much rather have my doll. And Betty was very lonely before Noni came."

Mama smiled and tucked a scarf around Rebecca's collar.

As the three of them walked to church, Rebecca said, "Mama, I used to make a mark in the back of my notebook for each week Papa was in jail. But it's taking so long . . . I've stopped now."

Mama took Rebecca's hand and held it tight. "I

know, little one. I was just thinking how cold it must be for him in that prison."

"We must pray for him," Granny said.

The cold wind stung Rebecca's eyes. But she said to herself, "I *won't* cry."

❧ IT WAS too windy to play up on the bare winter *koppies*.

"Don't sit about all by yourself, child," Granny would reprimand Rebecca. "There are the girls playing hopscotch across the road. Put on your jacket and go on out."

Rebecca joined her school friends' games now. But it saddened her not having a best friend.

One Thursday Mama came home with a doll's pram for her. Mama's madam had been clearing out Mandy's toy closet and had told her to take anything she wanted before the gardener carted it all away to the rubbish bin. Most of the toys were broken or had parts missing, Mama said, but the pram was in good condition except for one wheel bent out of shape. There was even a fitted mattress and a blanket and pillow.

Granny cut some doll's sheets out of an old pillowcase, and Rebecca put both her dolls in the pram, side by side, and took them for a walk up and down the road outside her house. She hoped that some of her friends would come by so she could show the pram to them. The bent wheel made it rattle and squeak noisily, but Rebecca didn't mind. She thought the pram with its pink-painted wickerwork was beautiful. Her dolls didn't have to sleep in cardboard boxes any more.

She pushed them along until she came to the end of the block of houses, then turned and went back in the direction of the church and the bus station. Mr. Lekota came striding along, the wind tugging at the skirts of his robe, the round toes of his stubbed black boots covered in the red dust of the road.

"Taking your baby for a walk, Rebecca. That's nice." He peered under the hood. "Oh—I see you have two babies—a black one and a white one." He chuckled. "I hope they are good friends."

"Yes, Mr. Lekota," Rebecca said shyly.

"Good. Good. God bless you, child." He patted her head and turned into an alley that ran between the blocks of houses.

At the bus station the first of the late-afternoon buses and *kombis* were pulling up, dropping passengers off before turning to go back into town. The wind gusted, sending dust and dry leaves swirling about. Rebecca, with only a sweater over her short cotton dress, shivered. She tucked her dolls in firmly under the blanket and turned to go home.

Above the squeak and clatter of the pram's wheels on the rutted road, she heard footsteps behind her. They were quick and were gaining on her. She hurried along faster, hearing the footsteps closer. In the light of the sinking sun a long shadow was thrown flat along the road beside the dolls' pram. Her heart gave a start of fear—the *tsotsis*; she was passing the alley where they always hung about. She felt a hand on her shoulder. She was still a good distance from her front gate; freeing her shoulder she started to run with the pram, but the hand restrained her again.

"Rebecca," a voice said. The hand on her shoulder felt gentle. She looked up. A tall, thin man was looking down at her. He was smiling. "Rebecca," he said, "don't run away from me."

She stared. The man's presence beside her was so unexpected that for a moment she was confused. Then his voice, his features all came together in a familiar shape. *"Papa,"* she whispered. She put out her hand and touched the cloth of his trousers to feel if it really was he, standing there, beside her on the road.

"It really is me, little one." He stooped and lifted her up, holding her tightly to him.

"Papa—they've let you go—they've let you go," she whispered again and again.

He didn't answer. She moved her head back a little so that she could look at him. He was smiling, smiling, as the tears ran down his cheeks. "Come," he said, putting her down. "Let's go home." He pulled a large blue handkerchief from his pocket and blew his nose, then took her by the hand.

Pushing the dolls' pram with the other hand, she walked home, she and Papa together.

"Lucky it's Thursday," she told him. "Mama's home."

"Thursday. Oh, good! I was released just this afternoon without any warning, and I didn't even remember what day it is."

"Mama brought me this dolls' pram today. Look, Papa, I have two dolls now."

He stopped and peered into the pram. "A white one—and a black one too!"

"Auntie Miriam bought the black one for me. Her name is Noni. I'll show her to you when we get inside."

"What a noise this pram makes," Papa said. "I see one of the back wheels is crooked. Tomorrow, I'll straighten it out for you, and we'll oil it; then it will ride smoothly and your dollies won't get shaken about."

When the front gate squeaked as they went through it, he said, "The gate needs a drop of oil too."

"YOU GO in first," Papa whispered at the front door. "Don't say anything."

Rebecca went in, pulling the pram up over the doorstep. Granny, her back to the door, was scraping carrots. Mama, on the couch in the corner, was mending a hole John had torn in his jacket.

"I was coming to get you," Mama said without

looking up. "It's too cold to be outside dressed like that."

Quietly, Papa stepped in behind Rebecca, holding a finger to his lips. Smiling, they stood together in silence. Mama looked up. For a moment she was speechless. Then her sewing fell to the floor and she gave a great cry like the sound of a seabird. Granny turned. In a few strides Papa was across the room, Mama sobbing in his arms. John, hearing her cry, came dashing out of the bedroom. It took a few seconds for him to realize what was happening, then he seemed to fly across the room toward Papa, who looked into his face and embraced him. Rebecca went and wriggled her way in among them, feeling the closeness of their warm bodies, tasting the salt of the tears that were falling.

Knife in one hand, carrot in the other, Granny watched, her cheeks glistening with tears, shaking her head in disbelief.

"You're so thin," Mama kept saying, "so thin."

"How could I eat that horrible prison food when I'm so used to Granny's good cooking," Papa teased.

Rebecca thought how strange it was that in all the long months of trouble and loneliness she had never once seen Mama in tears; and now that Papa was home it seemed she couldn't stop crying.

"THE CHILDREN have grown," Papa remarked at the supper table.

"Seven months make a big difference," Auntie

141

Miriam said. She had come in from work and screamed at the sight of Papa sitting in his favorite chair. All through the meal she chattered steadily.

"Seven months is the blink of an eye compared with Nelson Mandela's twenty-seven years in prison," Papa said gravely.

"Does *he* have children?" Rebecca asked.

"Children. Grandchildren."

"They should let him out too, Papa," she said.

"I just wish I'd had a piece of meat to cook tonight," Granny said.

"If only I'd known they were letting you out," Mama lamented, "I'd have borrowed money from my madam and got something at the butcher."

"Nothing could taste better than eating *putu* here, at my own table, with my own family around me. I can't tell you how much I dreamed about it in that jail."

"And you didn't even know they were letting you go?" John asked.

"No. Even our lawyers didn't know. The guard came and took me from the cell. I thought I was going for questioning again. They said nothing. They gave me back my things and led me to this big wooden door. Another guard unlocked it, and there I was, out on the street. Buses, and people walking along. I thought I was dreaming. But I didn't have the money for bus fare. So I walked to the office of the committee that helps political prisoners. Big Albert told me about them when we shared a cell for a while. When I got there, they told me that all of us had been released, except for Big Albert."

"*Hau!*" Granny shook her head gravely; Auntie Miriam groaned out loud.

"He'll have to stand trial?" John asked.

Papa nodded. "It makes me feel bad—to be free while he's still inside."

"What about those three lawyers?" Mama asked. "Won't they defend him?"

"They'll do whatever can be done," Papa said.

Rebecca finished her food and wriggled onto Papa's lap. With his arms about her, she felt content.

EARLY NEXT morning Mama pulled on her coat and went to the public phone at the bus station to call her madam. She told her she wouldn't be back until Monday, as she wanted to spend some time with her husband. "She was glad to hear you were out of jail," she said to Papa, "but she wasn't too pleased that I've decided to take a few days off." Mama shrugged, and laughed.

"Let her do the work for herself for a change," John said. "She might as well get some practice. She needs to be ready for the time when black people are running this country."

"You always say that, Johnny—but *when* will that be?" Rebecca asked her brother.

"Soon," he said.

"It will take a while yet, son," Papa told him. "Maybe by the time you children are grown up."

"That's too long to wait," John answered. "You'll see, Papa—it's coming sooner than you think. Why is the government letting us use the beaches now? Because they're beginning to understand at last that we are *demanding* equal treatment. So they throw us a crumb here, a crumb there. But it's not enough. We won't be satisfied so long as five million whites are telling twenty-eight million blacks what they are allowed to do and not do. It's not right. It's going to change, Papa."

But Rebecca was worried about what was happening now. "Maybe your madam will be mad at you for not coming to work and you'll lose your job, Mama."

Mama laughed again. "Don't worry your head about that, little one. My madam needs me. She'll never let me go. Without me she wouldn't be able to find where anything is in the kitchen."

"But what will she do?" Rebecca asked. She was thinking of that big white kitchen without Mama in charge.

"They'll just go out and eat in restaurants every night until I get back," Mama said. "It's time to go to school now, children. Hurry along, little one. Tell Miss Molefe our good news, that Papa is *home*!"

ON MONDAY Papa returned to work. His boss paid him part of the week's wages in advance, and that night he came home with a bag of groceries and kerosene for the heater. Soon the house was warm again and Rebecca's stomach felt full. Granny cooked extra food and asked John to take it around to Big Albert's family.

In the days that followed, Rebecca began to forget about the cold, hungry time of Papa's imprisonment, the loneliness, the sadness. Together she and he fixed the pram and oiled the gate. But in the village, the buzz of talk about the removal was at the back of all the ordinary things that went on each day. Sometimes the snakes slid again into Rebecca's dreams: Once she was showing Noni the dolls in the pram, but under the covers they found snakes instead, and she cried out in her sleep.

Spring breezes blowing over the *veld* started to warm the days. The jacaranda dappled the yard in blue-mauve shade; the blossoms drifted down, leaving the tree dark green and feathery-leaved.

In the new school year, Rebecca moved up to a higher grade. She was glad Miss Molefe would be teaching them again.

John's class continued out in the school yard under the trees. "We have to share books because there aren't enough to go around," he complained. "They want to keep us as miserable as possible to force us to move."

ONE EVENING Auntie Miriam came home waving the newspaper, spilling over with her news before she was in through the door. The three lawyers, she announced, were appealing to the planning department to change the ruling so the village would not be declared a "black spot," and to grant the villagers the right to remain in their homes. The paper reported that since people all over the world had learned about the removal and the arrests, letters, telegrams, and messages of all kinds had been coming into the country, urging the government not to uproot the villagers from the place that was theirs.

The magic eye of the television, Rebecca thought to herself as the grown-ups discussed the news; *maybe it is going to save us. . . .*

ON A Saturday morning in late summer, Rebecca was sitting at the kitchen table untangling a ball of pink yarn. Granny was teaching her to crochet. But the doll's blanket she was working on was going very slowly.

Papa was at work. John was out. Auntie Miriam was standing on a chair while Granny pinned up the hem of a dress she was making for her. Bright sunshine filled the room, and in the yard birds twittered and sang in the jacaranda tree.

Rebecca pulled and hooked the yarn through the looped stitches. Beyond the murmur of the women's conversation, the sounds of a disturbance outside began to drift into the house. She looked up. Through the open window she saw people scurrying outdoors, a crowd forming in the road, heard loud voices rising.

146

"What's all the fuss about?" Auntie Miriam asked. "Rebecca, run outside and see what's happening."

"You stay right where you are, child," Granny told her. "I don't want you outside if there's trouble."

The door was flung open and John rushed in. "Have you heard! Have you heard!" He was gasping, out of breath, hardly able to speak.

"John—what is it!" Granny scolded. "You've given me such a fright I nearly swallowed a pin."

"Heard *what*, Johnny?" Auntie Miriam asked.

"*Mandela*. They're letting him out of jail!"

"I've heard that before," Granny said. "But it's never happened."

"Granny. This time it's *true*. They're letting him out. *Tomorrow*. I've just heard it on the radio at Joshua's house. I ran all the way home. It's true, Granny. *Tomorrow*."

"Tomorrow!" Auntie Miriam shrieked. She stepped down off the chair, picked up Rebecca, and danced around the room with her, the yarn trailing behind them.

"Auntie Miriam—the pins in your dress are pricking me," Rebecca protested, laughing.

Granny picked up the ball of yarn, muttering as she wound it up, "Thank God . . . oh, thank God . . ."

WHEN MAMA, weighed down with packages, walked unexpectedly in the next morning, Rebecca wished that the happiness in their house could go on forever, the smiling, the laughter, the excitement, the cheerful voices.

"I told my madam," Mama announced, "even though it's not my Sunday off, 'Ma'm, today I will be celebrating our leader's release at home with my own people.' Nanny and the gardener also went off."

"Did she mind?" John asked.

Mama shrugged. "Who knows? She said they're going to be watching on the television this afternoon."

"Worldwide attention," Rebecca said, and everyone laughed.

"Oh." Papa shook his head in wonder. "Truly, the whole world will be watching today as our leader comes back to us. You know, Mama," he added as he took her bundles from her, "maybe this boy of ours is right after all. Maybe our freedom is coming sooner than I ever thought."

In the afternoon, at the hour when Mandela was to walk out of prison, it seemed as if the whole village was a party. Everyone was out wherever there was space to gather. This time Mama allowed Rebecca to join the crowds. "It's different now," she explained. "You'll come to no harm. This is a rejoicing crowd."

Under the bright, joyful banners, among the dancing, the chanting, cheering, smiling villagers, Rebecca felt as if they were all being carried along by a great wave of good feeling. It was as if the happiness she had felt when Papa came home from jail, and when Auntie Miriam had brought her the black doll, and the wonder of the magician's magic, were spread out among all the people dancing under the hot, blue sky. If only Noni could be here too, she thought.

"OH," Auntie Miriam moaned that night when the celebrations were over, "I wish my sister hadn't listened to those baboons who kept coming to our house and telling us how wonderful it was going to be at Pofadderkloof. The house hasn't been bull-dozed, even though the planning committee told us it would be. There it stands, empty next door; and there *they* are—with all the children miserable and hungry and lonely, far away in that place, in the middle of nowhere."

She must have thought about it all night. More than once Rebecca heard Auntie Miriam groan as she turned and tossed restlessly on the mattress on the floor. Next morning at breakfast she announced, *"I've made up my mind.* D'you know what I've decided to do? And no one can stop me!" Leaning forward she grasped the edge of the table. *"I'm taking the bus to Pofadderkloof.* I'm telling my sister that now Mandela is free, things are going to change for us. And I'm bringing them back with me from that miserable place."

They were all silent with amazement.

"Well—what do you think of that!" she said.

"You'll bring Noni back!" Rebecca cried.

"Of course, child!" Auntie Miriam laughed. "Do you think I'll leave her there—in the middle of nowhere? I'm going to bring them all back to the *middle of somewhere!*" Her dimples came and went and she slid her clinking bracelets up and down her arm, smiling and nervous, as if she was waiting for someone to try and stop her.

"But Miriam," Papa began. "It's not decided yet. Everyone hopes the bulldozers aren't coming. But maybe they will. Wouldn't it be better to wait and see what will happen?"

"Don't worry, Papa," John told him. "They won't have the nerve to start bulldozing now. The whole world is watching. I tell you, Papa—*we are not going to be moved.*"

Rebecca watched her brother.

Auntie Miriam listened to him as if a grown-up were talking. "Maybe you're right, Johnny," she said. "Whatever happens, it's better for them to be here, home, among their own people. This way we can all support each other. My mind is made up. On Saturday I'm going. To fetch them back."

REBECCA wanted to see Auntie Miriam off. Though it was not yet light, Granny was up making tea for them. In the night Rebecca had decided on a present to send to Noni: one of the bear books. Now Auntie Miriam slipped it into her nylon bag and zipped it up firmly, ready to go. It was still too early for the first bus into town, where she'd pick up another bus headed toward Pofadderkloof, but she was impatient to leave. "If I don't manage to thumb a lift, it's a long walk from where the second bus drops me," she told them.

Rebecca got dressed, tucked her dolls into the pram, and went with Auntie Miriam out into the dark dawn. Pushing the pram, she had to hurry to keep pace with Auntie Miriam's quick step. Lamps were already lit in many of the houses as people readied for the long journey to work. The air smelled fresh and new, and a hush lay over the village. A fiery flare rimmed the edge of the dark *veld* as the night slowly brightened into day.

"Don't tell Noni about my new doll. Or about the pram. I want to surprise her when she comes home."

"I'll keep your secret," Auntie Miriam assured her. "Don't worry."

She waited with Auntie Miriam as a line formed at the bus stop. At last, headlights swept over the sleepy, patient faces of the waiting passengers as the bus pulled into the square.

"Good-bye, little one," Auntie Miriam said as she boarded the bus. "It won't be long before your best friend is back. See you soon."

"Good-bye, Auntie Miriam. Go well. See you soon." Rebecca waited until her face appeared, framed in the lighted window.

The bus backed up, slowly turned, then lumbered off. At the window, Auntie Miriam waved and smiled. Rebecca waved back, kept waving, until the red tail lights of the bus were swallowed up in the foggy dawn.

Perhaps when Mama came home on Thursday the house next door would no longer be empty. Perhaps Noni would be there again.

As Rebecca pushed her pram back home the sun rose up over the dark *koppies*. In the yard the branches of the jacaranda were black against the clear light of the dawn sky. In the summers to come, when the tree hung heavy again with blue flowers, perhaps she and Noni would be sitting in its shade, taking turns to play with the two dolls.

Glossary of South African words

Amandla!   Power! Rallying cry of the Freedom Movement.

Kombi(s)   Minibus(es) used to transport black workers to and from town.

Hau!   Exclamation of surprise.

Koppie(s)   Hill(s).

Mealies   Ears of corn.

Mealie meal   Cornmeal.

Nkosi Sikalel' iAfrika   The black South African anthem.

Pofadder   Puff adder snake.

Putu   Porridge made of white cornmeal—staple food of black South Africans.

Rand   South African money.

Tsotsi(s)	Young delinquents who rob and threaten black communities.
Veld	Open, rolling grassland.
Xhosa	Language of one of the South African tribes.